YES REHEARSAL

THE ROMANTICS
BOOK THREE

KELLY BRIGHT

CHAPTER 1

ELLA

"Are you for real?" I mutter under my breath, my hand pausing midair as I catch sight of him. The glass of whiskey smash I'd been cradling almost tumbles out of my grasp onto the worn concrete below. My heart revs into overdrive, pounding inside my chest. "This can't be happening."

Especially now. When I'm fasting.

I don't mean fasting from food. Or alcohol. I'm fasting from men. From sex. From the meaningless trysts that have become my usual. It was the recent engagement of my two best friends, Rosie and Clara, that helped me realize I want more.

So, I'm dating, in earnest. I want to get to know someone and cultivate a connection that goes beyond the physical.

Apparently, the universe has a wicked sense of humor.

Even from this distance, I recognize that deep

brown hair, now a little shorter, a little more styled. The way he carries himself, a touch more rigid, the nervousness clear in his darting glances around the bar. I hadn't thought I would ever see him again, and certainly not here, in Nashville's bustling downtown, a world away from our shared past. But here he is, and every ounce of air is sucked out of my lungs as if he still has that power over me.

Mark Dane. It's been ... what? Eight years? Maybe nine?

The details are fuzzy, lost to a haze of time and heartbreak. But the face? That's seared into my memory, and it's not something I could forget even if I tried. I've held that face, kissed that face, and stared at that face for hours on end. I know it as well as my own.

I suddenly feel like I'm coming undone.

It's a warm evening in Music City, and the rooftop bar of the trendy Second Avenue restaurant is buzzing with life. The lights of Nashville are spread out before me, a vibrant canvas of colors against the twilight sky. There's an energy in the air, a mix of chatter, clinking glasses, and the soft strumming of a nearby guitar. So Nashville.

But as I sit here alone at this tiny table on the corner of the roof, the city's allure fades into the background. All I can focus on is the man who's just walked in.

My mind races, trying to process the information, to comprehend the sight before me. I blink, hard, hoping the vision of him will vanish like a mirage. But he doesn't. Instead, he moves further into the bar, his eyes skimming over the crowd, unaware of my presence.

I came here tonight, ready for an adventure, prepared to dive headfirst into the world of online dating. The new frontier. After all, it's the twenty-first century, and I'm a woman on a mission. A mission to find something real, something lasting, something that isn't just another wild fling or a one-night stand.

But this? This was not what I'd bargained for.

Hold it together, I tell myself. *You're a grown woman with a successful career. He can't hurt you anymore. That's ancient history.*

My phone chimes softly, breaking the thread of my thoughts. It's a message from InnerWisdom615, my MindMate date. He's running late, he says, delayed by his niece's school play. A sense of irony washes over me, a cruel joke by the universe. Here I am, waiting for my mystery man while my past struts into the bar like he owns the place.

Swiping the message away, I set my phone down and take a sip of my drink, the ice clinking against the glass. The whiskey burns a trail down my throat. The sharp taste anchors me to the present. My hand shakes slightly, betraying my inner turmoil. I lower the glass and stare at it, my mind spinning with a thousand questions.

I'm still in shock. How is it possible that after all these years, I end up in the same bar, on the same night, waiting for a date, and in walks Mark? It feels like a sick twist of fate, or a cosmic joke of some sort.

I don't know whether to laugh or cry.

I swallow hard, steeling myself. I have no idea what this night has in store for me, but whatever happens next, I'm not the same girl Mark left behind all those years ago.

Not even close. My best friends, Rosie and Clara, can attest to that. They watched and offered their support through the ups and the downs. They know I'm different now. Although honestly, I'm not sure if it's all for the better.

I push my conflicted thoughts away, as best I can. I suppose there will be time to ruminate later. Not here. Not now.

One more gulp of the whiskey, and I'm ready. Ready for whatever this night throws my way. The echoes of the past might have knocked the wind out of me, but I'm not out of the fight. Not yet.

As I take one more glance at Mark, now engrossed in a quiet conversation with the bartender, a sense of determination washes over me. Bring it on, universe. I've got my armor on, and I'm ready for battle. With that thought, I sit up straighter in my chair, crossing my legs, the silky material of my skirt brushing against my skin.

Taking a deep breath, I turn my gaze away from him, reaching for my phone once more. The message from InnerWisdom615 is still there, a lifeline to normalcy amidst the whirlwind of my emotions. And though part of me screams to bolt, to escape the chaos threatening to consume me, I remind myself why I'm here.

I came for a date. A chance at love. A step forward into my future. And even though my past just strutted through the door, I'm not going to let it stop me.

I'm Ella Lovelace, and I don't run from challenges. I face them head-on.

Picking up my phone, I type out a quick response to InnerWisdom615, assuring him that I'm still here, still waiting. I hit send, taking one last look at the man from my past, then turning my attention back to the city skyline.

Tonight's adventure might have just taken an unexpected turn, but I'm still keen to see how my MindMate date goes. After all, this could be the date that changes my entire life. The app's focus is on making connections by getting to know each other on an intellectual level appealed to me.

I desperately want—maybe even need—to connect on a deeper, intellectual level. I joke around and pretend like I'm all about the physical when it comes to my men-of-the-moment, but it's an act.

Nothing more.

Shh, don't tell anyone.

I settle back into my chair, sipping my whiskey, the anticipation for the night ahead buzzing under my skin. As the echoes of Mark Dane's arrival begin to recede, I remind myself that this is my story. And no one, not even a ghost from my past, is going to stand in my way.

A half-hour slips by, the minutes ticking away as I wait for my elusive date, the man hidden behind the screen name of InnerWisdom615. I distract myself by people-watching, my gaze skimming over the crowd, drinking in the sights and sounds of Nashville nightlife.

The buzz of conversation is punctuated by bursts of laughter, the clinking of glasses, and the happy guitar. The city is alive, and the rooftop bar is a microcosm of that life, brimming with energy and stories waiting to be told.

Tonight, my story is one of waiting. Waiting for a man I've never met. Waiting for a chance at a fresh start.

Suddenly, my phone lights up, a message from InnerWisdom615 flashing across the screen. He's close, he says, promising to be there soon. My pulse quickens at the prospect of meeting him, but my gaze keeps straying back to the man who is etched deep into my past.

Mark.

He's found a table across the bar, seated with a beer in his hand, his attention fixed on the Nashville skyline.

I turn away, refocusing my own attention on the task at hand. I pull out a compact mirror from my purse, checking my makeup for any signs of smearing or fading. Satisfied with what I see, I reapply a layer of my favorite pink lipstick, press my lips together, and tuck the mirror back into my purse.

A quick scan of the bar confirms Mark is still there, lost in his thoughts. The sight of him throws me back into the past, a past filled with lazy summer days and stolen kisses on Long Island. It's hard to reconcile the man I see now with the college boy who was part of my life one memorable summer.

He's changed, and grown. I can tell. But so have I.

With a deep breath, I push those thoughts away, focusing on the here and now. I order another drink, the familiar burn of whiskey giving me a dose of much-needed courage.

The minutes pass like molasses, stretching out into an eternity. My phone buzzes again. InnerWisdom615. He's arrived, he says. He's wearing a green tie and a hat. My eyes scan the crowd, searching for a man matching the description. And then I see him, stepping out of the elevator, the hat in question perched on his head. My breath hitches in my chest.

He's handsome, with a rugged charm about him. He scans the room, his eyes landing on me. A warm smile stretches across his face as he makes his way toward my table. As he approaches, I stand, extending a hand towards him. He takes it, his handshake firm, his smile widening.

"Ella?" he asks, his voice rich, filled with warmth.

"Yes," I reply, giving him a welcoming smile. "You must be InnerWisdom615."

He chuckles, a light, pleasant sound. "Please, call me Wes."

Wes. The name seems to fit him. As we sit down, I can't help but be intrigued. He's not what I expected, but then again, I didn't know what to expect.

He starts the conversation by apologizing for his tardiness, explaining about his niece's play in more detail. It's endearing, the way he talks about her with such affection. As we continue to chat, I find myself genuinely enjoying his company. He's charming, funny, and attentive. There's an ease about him, a comfort that seeps into our conversation. But even as we talk, even as I laugh at his jokes, my mind keeps wandering back to the man across the bar.

Mark.

Why is he here? And why tonight of all nights? I try to push the thoughts away, but they creep back in, persistent and demanding.

Mark Dane, the ghost from my past, has walked back into my life, and I have no idea why.

As the night progresses, I manage to keep my attention on Wes, making sure to ask him about his interests, his work, his life. He's an open book, offering glimpses into his world. But even as we converse, even as I find myself charmed by his stories, I can't help but wonder about the chapters of my own life that were left unwritten.

The sight of Mark in the bar has unmoored something within me, stirring up memories I thought were buried deep. As much as I focus on Wes, as much as I am drawn to his easy charm and genuine demeanor, I can't help but feel the pull of the past.

I may not know why Mark is here or what brought him to Nashville, but I can't deny the fact that his presence has shaken me. And as the night draws on, as I continue to engage with Wes, a part of me realizes that this isn't a simple coincidence. It's a sign, a message from the universe that it's time to confront my past, to deal with the unfinished business that's been lurking in the shadows.

As Wes and I share a dessert, a chocolate lava cake that he insisted we try, I decide that whatever happens tonight, whatever curveballs life throws my way, I'll face them. The past may have walked back into my life in the form of Mark Dane, but I'm not the same girl who fell for him all those years ago.

With that thought in mind, I turn my attention back to Wes, ready to embrace whatever this night has in store for me. But as I listen to his stories, as I laugh at his jokes, I can't help but wonder what tomorrow will bring. The first chapter of my new life has started with a twist, but I'm ready to dive headfirst into the rest of the story, whatever it may be.

As the night stretches on, the rooftop bar gradually fills with people. The hum of conversation, the laughter, the clinking of glasses—they all contribute to the palpable energy of the place. Amidst the crowd, I am with Wes, but my mind often veers towards the man who's been a constant presence across the room.

Mark Dane.

As we dive into our decadent dessert, I notice Wes glancing over his shoulder, his eyes narrowing on a figure across the room. Following his gaze, my heart tightens when I realize he's looking at Mark. There's a moment of unspoken understanding between us.

He's recognized Mark Dane, the soccer star. Only I don't realize that fact yet.

"Didn't know we were in the company of a celebrity tonight," Wes comments lightly, trying to hide his star-struck expression behind a casual smile.

I nod, trying to catch up and feigning surprise, "Seems like it."

Our conversation shifts from personal anecdotes to Mark's soccer career. I had no idea that my old flame played professionally, let alone for Nashville's team. It's a surreal experience, discussing Mark in third person with Wes, a man who doesn't know about my history with the renowned soccer player.

As we speak, I steal glances at Mark. He's engaged in an animated conversation with a woman by his side. Seeing him with her sparks a pang of something I refuse to analyze. I swallow it down, chasing the uncomfortable feeling with a sip of whiskey.

Over the next hour, Wes and I navigate around a multitude of topics. We discuss everything from our favorite books to our views on current world events. He's incredibly intelligent, his insights reflective of a mind that constantly seeks knowledge. MindMate did a good job, matching up together. With him, the conversation flows easily. He has a knack for making me feel comfortable and seen.

Still, Mark's presence persists in the back of my mind, an uninvited guest.

Then, as Wes delves into a humorous tale from his college years, I see Mark stand from his seat, his eyes scanning the room. My heart lurches as his gaze lands on me, a flicker of recognition flashing across his face.

The world seems to slow as our eyes lock across the crowded rooftop. He gives a small nod of acknowledgment, a ghost of a smile tugging at his lips. And just like that, I'm back on Long Island, reliving memories I'd locked away in the deepest corners of my mind.

The sound of Wes' laughter brings me back to reality. I force a smile onto my face, returning my attention to Wes, the man who's been nothing but charming and understanding tonight. I shove the thoughts of Mark aside, reminding myself to stay in the present.

For the rest of the evening, I try my best to focus on Wes. I laugh at his jokes, share some of my own stories, and enjoy the delectable food. All the while, a part of me remains hyper-aware of Mark's presence across the room.

Damn him.

Eventually, as the night draws to a close, Wes and I stand. He walks me towards the elevator, thanking me for a wonderful evening. He is a true gentleman, his actions reflecting a sincere respect for me. I assure him that the pleasure was all mine, and I mean it. Despite the unexpected surprise, it had been a delightful evening.

As we descend in the elevator, my mind begins to race. This was supposed to be a simple date. A chance to meet someone new, to maybe start over. But life had thrown me a curveball.

Mark Dane, the boy I spent an unforgettable summer with all those years ago, has re-entered my life.

I step out of the elevator and say my goodbyes to Wes, promising to text him soon. He leaves me with a warm smile, but the moment he's out of sight, my thoughts shift back to Mark.

He's still upstairs. I could leave now and avoid him. Or I could face the past head-on.

I weigh my options for a moment. Running away from this won't erase the past or how we left things.

I know what I need to do.

I turn back towards the elevator. I press the button

for the rooftop bar and feel the slow ascent. As the elevator doors open, I step out, bracing myself for the reunion that awaits me. It's time to face Mark Dane, not as the young girl I was then, but as the woman I am now.

I have questions, and it's high time I got some answers.

CHAPTER 2

ELLA

"Well, well, well, Ella Lovelace, alive and in the flesh. What are the chances?" Mark's voice is smooth as butter, startlingly familiar yet laced with a hint of surprise.

His grin is as dazzling as I remember, matching the spark in his magnetic blue eyes.

I could lose myself in those eyes. Correction: I *have* lost myself in those eyes. Many, many times. They're dreamy, and that's putting it mildly.

"I could ask you the same, Mark Dane," I retort, trying to steady my swirling thoughts.

This reunion is about as unexpected as a snowfall in July.

"Still as feisty as ever, I see." His laughter rings in my ears, bringing back a torrent of memories I thought were long buried.

His casual attire, a pair of well-worn jeans and a navy t-shirt, fits him like a glove, accentuating his toned physique. He looks the same, yet different. Older, more mature. But the same sparkle in his eyes, the same playful grin.

He's every bit as alluring as he was back when we were college kids, spending our summers on Long Island. Only it seems that he's gained a measure of confidence. Maybe becoming a professional soccer player helped him along in that department.

Makes sense.

"So, what brings you to Nashville?" I try to steer the conversation to safer waters.

"Work," he says vaguely, his eyes scanning the crowded rooftop bar. The city lights twinkle in his gaze, adding an extra layer of mystery to his already intriguing persona.

"Didn't think I'd run into you here. It's been what … eight years?"

He seems genuinely surprised to see me. It stings a little that he didn't keep track of me, considering how inseparable we were. But then again, I returned to Nashville right after college, eager to carve out a new identity away from the recent past, away from Mark.

I'd always known I'd return to Loveland—and my two best friends—once I completed my bachelor's degree in fashion design at Columbia University. I'd never even considered anything else.

Just as I'm about to respond, a waiter approaches our table. It's Johnny, a familiar face who knows my penchant for whiskey smashes. He gives me a sympathetic smile. "Another one, Ella?"

I glance at Mark, who's watching the exchange with

a bemused expression. "Make it two," I tell the waiter, feeling reckless.

I'm on an emotional rollercoaster and Mark Dane just happens to be my unexpected companion. This is not how I envisioned my evening. I'd expected nothing more than a pleasant, lighthearted date with InnerWisdom615.

Johnny nods and heads off, leaving me alone with Mark. We've a lot to catch up on. We have memories to relive, and maybe old wounds to heal.

That's a lot at once.

I know. No pressure, right?

I can't shake the feeling that the universe has a peculiar sense of humor, reuniting me with Mark on a night that was meant to be about new beginnings.

Is someone trying to tell me something? Should I pay attention and listen carefully? Or is this all just one huge coincidence?

As Mark's gaze meets mine, filled with warmth and a hint of amusement, I wonder if this could be a new beginning in itself. After all, Nashville is a city of music and magic, where unexpected reunions can perhaps lead to enchanting harmonies.

Right?

I'm getting all gooey inside. I tell myself to shake it off.

Seriously. Shake it off, Lovelace.

In the lull of the moment, with the city's nighttime symphony playing in the background, I make a decision. Tonight, I won't shy away from the past. Instead, I'll embrace it, beginning with the boy who loved me on

Long Island and somehow found me again in the heart of Music City.

Whatever happens, I'll be okay. *I am okay.*

"Eight years," I finally say, meeting Mark's eyes. "I guess we have a lot to catch up on."

He agrees, and we dive right in.

Our conversation flows easily, as if the eight-year gap is merely a blip. We talk about the weather, our jobs, his move to Nashville. We talk about everything, really, except the memories. We aren't ready to go there … yet.

"A professional soccer player, huh?" I say, a half smile playing on my lips as I recall his obsession with the sport during our shared summer. "I'm not surprised. You were always trying to perfect that Ronaldo-esque kick."

He chuckles, running his fingers through his cropped hair, which, under the warm lighting of the bar, looks more golden than brown. "Well, you know, I had to put those skills to good use. Besides, I'm set up with a pretty decent gig. It's not every day you get to be part of a team that fans love. Nashville SC is a good one. With my salary and endorsement deals, the pay isn't too shabby either."

He narrows his eyes when he says this, and I get the idea he's watching for my reaction. Is Mark Dane trying to impress me right now?

I smile, holding back a laugh. Being this close to him … smiling at him, talking with him … it's turning me on. A warm, familiar pressure builds between my legs. I cross them in an attempt to make it stop.

Mark was a sensuous lover. A giver. My body remembers.

"So, that's why you moved to Music City," I muse, picking at the garnish on my drink.

"Exactly. Though, I must admit, I didn't expect to find a familiar face in the crowd." His gaze intensifies as it meets mine, and for a moment, I see a glimmer of the boy who stole my heart one summer.

"You knew I was from around here," I say. "Is that what brought you? Did you take a job in Nashville so you could look for me?"

He stops, then takes a long, slow sip of his drink. "That's quite a question," he muses.

"I don't hear you saying no," I reply.

He grins, but doesn't answer. Instead, we move on … for now. I intend to ask again, at some point. I'd like to know if he's thought of me over the years.

As we reminisce and laugh about our younger selves, I feel a strange sense of déjà vu. It's almost as if we're two old friends catching up after years of distance and life getting in the way.

The nagging feeling of unfinished business is still there, though, lurking in the back of my mind.

Just as I'm about to broach the topic, a loud cheer erupts from a nearby table. We both turn to see a group of men toasting to a friend's recent engagement. Watching the camaraderie, I recall how Mark and I used to be the ones garnering attention with our playful banter and blatant flirting.

Suddenly, the memories flood back, the bitter outweighing the sweet. I'd never wanted that to end. I had been so enamored with that man. He was my every-thing. I was ready to make him my everything, for the rest of my life.

Mark must sense my mood shift because he lightly touches my hand, his thumb gently stroking my knuck-les. It's a small gesture, but it's enough to pull me back from the precipice of past heartaches.

"Are you okay, Ella?" His voice is low, filled with concern. "I completely understand if this is over-whelming for you. You don't have to put on a brave face. It's emotional for me, too."

I glance at him, and despite the surprise of our unex-pected reunion, I can't deny the comfort his presence brings. His hand on mine feels like heaven. "Yeah, I'm good," I assure him, offering a small smile to drive home my point.

"Good," he echoes, his smile lighting up his face, making his eyes twinkle in the dim lighting.

We share another round of drinks, and as the night deepens, I realize this encounter is the furthest thing from a coincidence. It's as if we were meant to recon-nect, to open up old wounds and hopefully find a way to heal them.

At least, that's what I tell myself. My emotions are oscillating from one moment to the next. I can't seem to stop them doing so.

As the night draws to a close, I find myself blissfully lost in conversation, laughter, and shared memories with Mark Dane. This impromptu reunion isn't what I'd envi-sioned for my night, but maybe it's exactly what I needed.

Could this be a shot at a new beginning? Do I *want* a shot at a new beginning? Or is that just asking for trouble?

"I guess we should wrap this up," Mark says, glancing at his watch. "It's pretty late. I have training in the morning."

"Right," I agree, though a part of me is reluctant to call it a night. It feels like we're on the cusp of something—a resolution, a revival maybe—something significant.

But all that will have to wait. I have a busy day at work tomorrow, too.

The night is ending, and with it, the first chapter of our renewed … what? Acquaintanceship? Is that even a word?

We say our goodbyes, leaving me with a lingering sense of hope for what the future may hold.

I'll admit it … I'm interested. My body is most certainly interested. It's practically lit like a firecracker right now, desperate for Mark's touch. That man used to play my body like it was an instrument and he was the most skilled musician in the whole entire world. A shiver—the good kind—runs down my spine just thinking about it.

Who knew a mediocre blind date would lead to a night of reminiscing and reconnecting with an old flame? Life sure can surprise you.

Perhaps this reunion is the start of a new chapter in both our lives. But for now, all I can do is wait and see how things unfold.

I can't rush this. I definitely can't force it. That's no good, and would probably end badly.

Like it did last time.

Ugh.

When Mark finally stands to go, he does so with a lingering smile and an invitation to catch up again soon. I watch him leave the rooftop bar, his tall figure merging with the thrumming Nashville nightlife. My heart beats a steady rhythm in my chest—a mix of anticipation and nostalgia.

For a moment, I imagine myself getting caught up in the whirlwind that is Mark Dane all over again. It's exciting to think about how the two of us might be together here in Nashville. Instead of swimming and boating on the beaches of New York, maybe we could hike the hills of Tennessee. But I push those thoughts aside. I've got my life in Loveland, a thriving career, and my best friends.

Everything I need, I suppose.

After paying the tab, I leave the bar, my steps matching the rhythm of the city's beating heart. The night air is warm against my skin, and Downtown Nashville's vibrant energy is contagious. Even with the whirlwind of thoughts swirling in my head, I'm excited about the future.

Who knows? Maybe Music City will play a lovely symphony for me after all.

As I walk down Second Avenue amongst the tourists and partygoers, I pull out my phone to check for any missed messages. There, amidst the clutter of unread emails and social media notifications, is a message from

InnerWisdom615. I open it, reading the apologetic text from when he was running late. I can't help but chuckle.

Poor guy. He has no idea the significance of what just happened after he left the bar. How can he compete?

I type out a quick response, telling him that it's okay. Things happen. I don't mention my unexpected reunion. That's a story for another time. Wes doesn't need to know about Mark just yet. Or ever. I suppose that depends on how I want to play this.

As I reach my townhouse back home in Loveland, my mind is still on the evening's events. The last few hours have been nothing short of a roller coaster ride. An ordinary blind date turned into a surprise reunion with an old flame.

Life truly has a funny way of throwing curveballs. But isn't that what makes it interesting?

I climb the steps to my townhouse, a whirlwind of thoughts filling my head. As I unlock the door and step inside, I glance at my phone, the screen displaying a new message notification … from Mark. I grin as I read his text, a simple 'It was good to see you, Ella. Let's do it again soon.'

I stare at the screen for a moment, my heart fluttering at the prospect of seeing him again.

Hell.

I quickly push those feelings aside. After all, there's a lot to process. I can't forget that I have a life here in Loveland. A life that doesn't involve Mark Dane. At least, not yet. I can't seem too eager. I can't be too eager.

I'm not simply waiting around for him. I won't do that, now or ever. A lot would need to be done to get me over the heartbreak I experienced at his hands.

When Mark broke up with me, I was devastated. I had the distinct sense that he didn't want to do it. Like his hand was being forced. Still, though, he made his choice. I'm not sure we can get over that.

With one last glance at my phone, I put it away and head to my bedroom, the events of the night still replaying in my mind. As I fall into bed, I feel a sense of anticipation for what's to come.

Tonight was just the start. There's a whole new chapter waiting to unfold. Whether that chapter sees Mark and I back together or not remains to be seen. Perhaps we'll emerge as nothing but friends. Either way, I want resolution. It's always bothered me that we didn't really get that.

As I drift off to sleep, I think of Mark. Not the soccer star who's won over Nashville, but the boy from Long Island who won my heart all those summers ago.

It's been a long day, and tomorrow promises to be even longer. I've got back to back appointments at the boutique with barely enough time for a lunch break. But that's a problem for future Ella. Tonight, I'll let the memories of past summers and the anticipation of new beginnings lull me to sleep.

After all, tomorrow is another day, another chance for life to surprise me. Little do I know, it will do just that and more.

CHAPTER 3

ELLA

Sunlight breaches my blinds, casting my bedroom in soft, warm hues. I squint, burrowing further into my pillow as if that could stop the day from beginning.

Gonzo, my pet snake, is coiled happily in his habitat on the dresser. He'll need to be fed soon, but for now, he's docile. Resting like a baby.

My hand makes a blind journey to the nightstand, grappling for my phone.

I glance at the glowing screen, the brightness stinging my half-awake eyes. It's barely seven in the morning. But it's not the time that holds my attention—it's an unread message notification. From Mark.

All at once, last night comes crashing back: the unexpected reunion, the emotional whirlwind, the way his eyes crinkled at the corners when he smiled. A part of me, maybe the sensible part, wants to ignore the message, even delete it and pretend it doesn't exist. But there's a louder part, a part that remembers the warmth of his smile and the twinkle in his eyes under the dim bar lights.

Sitting up, I brace myself for a surge of emotions before clicking on his message. The words on the screen are casual and friendly—something about meeting for coffee. No pressure, no expectations. Just coffee.

A sense of relief washes over me. Mark is willing to talk, willing to let the past be past. And he's here, in Nashville. My city. For now, at least.

I start typing a reply, all business but with a dash of humor, "Sure, but only if you promise not to order a raspberry syrup frappuccino. Can't be seen with anyone who has such terrible taste in coffee."

I hit send, and my heart skips a beat. The ping seems deafening in the stillness of my room. I watch my screen, hardly daring to breathe. The reply comes almost instantly, assuring me he has "more sophisticated coffee tastes."

Chuckling, I slide out from under my sheets and get ready for the day, my mind buzzing with a cocktail of anticipation, excitement, and a tiny dash of anxiety. The coffee brewing in the kitchen fills my townhouse with its rich aroma. The cool hardwood floor under my bare feet, my favorite red mug heavy with hot coffee—each detail tethers me to the present.

But even as I head to my Ever After Bridals, my boutique, the summer breeze teasing through the open windows of my car, Mark and our upcoming coffee date hang over my thoughts.

Walking into my shop feels like stepping into a warm embrace. The familiar chatter and laughter of my team, the soft music playing in the background—it's all so soothingly normal, pulling me out of my reverie.

I love my work, and I'm proud of what my friends and I have built in The Romantics wedding services group. Our building is being remodeled, which will only make us more appealing to brides and grooms-to-be. Also, a TV production company is currently filming a docu-series about us. We don't know much yet about how it will turn out, but we're hopeful that being featured will elevate the visibility of our businesses. Since I design bridal gowns in addition to owning the boutique, whatever exposure comes from the docu-series stands to benefit me ... maybe most of all. I'm incredibly excited.

The day whizzes by in a blur of customers and appointments, each one keeping my mind off Mark. By the time I check my phone again, I see he has responded to my earlier text, assuring me again he has "better taste than a raspberry frappuccino." His light-hearted banter makes me laugh. We always did have a lot of fun together.

Life is so unpredictable. This bustling boutique, my date with Wes, AKA InnerWisdom615, the thrilling and terrifying prospect of reconnecting with Mark—it's a wild, reality-show-like whirlwind. It's my whirlwind, though, and I wouldn't have it any other way.

I think I might finally be getting somewhere. I can feel it in the tingle on the back of my neck. Although, granted, I have no idea where—or with whom—I'll end up. Something good must ultimately come from setting the intention though, right?

I'm in search of a love that's real.

Tucking my phone into my pocket, I throw myself back into my work. There are customers to help, a boutique to run, and a date to prepare for. For now, that's more than enough.

Before the day fully begins, I know I'm in for a rollercoaster. The boutique, though a source of joy and creativity for me, can sometimes feel like a battleground filled with laces and silks, colors and beads. Still, nothing compares to the euphoria of seeing a client's face light up when they find their perfect dress. It makes the chaos worth it.

When I enter the store, my eyes instantly find Becca Hamilton, my ever-dependable assistant, already moving with swift efficiency. A mousy-haired whirlwind, she's an organization goddess. With her assistance, I've turned this once fledgling boutique into Loveland's most popular bridal shop.

"Morning, Ella," Becca greets me with a beaming smile. "Your coffee is on the desk." As if I couldn't love her more.

With coffee in hand and Becca by my side, we tackle the day. Our first few appointments go smoothly, almost suspiciously so. The clients are polite, even amiable, and they're just as enthralled by the dresses as we are.

Our lunch break is quick and uneventful, a hurried sandwich at our desks. No one said running a successful boutique would include long, leisurely lunches. But as I've often reminded myself, I wouldn't trade it for anything else.

It's in the early afternoon that our most anticipated client of the day arrives. Stella Bennet, Loveland's leading socialite and a notoriously hard-to-please customer, graces us with her demanding presence. Stella's wedding is set to be the talk of the town, and every bridal shop in Loveland has been vying for the privilege of dressing her. She's chosen us, a testament to the growing reputation of our boutique.

Her arrival is preceded by a waft of expensive perfume, a scent that's as formidable as her personality. Becca and I exchange a knowing look before plastering on our most dazzling smiles.

"Welcome, Stella," I greet her, hoping my cheer doesn't come across as too strained.

The next few hours are a frenzy. Stella dismisses several dresses with a mere glance, her eyes sharp and critical. I feel my optimism slowly waning. But just as I'm beginning to lose hope, Stella steps out of the changing room in a stunning lace gown, her eyes shining with unshed tears.

"This is it," she whispers, her voice filled with emotion. "This is my wedding dress."

And this is what it's all about.

The relief that washes over me is indescribable. I share a victorious grin with Becca, who looks as relieved as I feel. As Stella admires herself in the mirror, a satisfied sigh escapes her.

"It's perfect," she murmurs. "Thank you."

"You're most welcome," I reply, a huge grin on my face. "It's our pleasure."

It truly is.

When Stella finally leaves, Becca and I collapse onto the chairs in the office. It's been a long day. But as I glance at the clock, I realize the day is far from over. I still have to meet Clara and Rosalie for dinner.

"Great job today," I say to Becca. "Why don't you head home? I'll close up."

She gives me a grateful smile before heading out the door. After she leaves, I begin the closing routine, my mind already drifting towards the comfort of dinner with my friends. The boutique's success has brought a lot of changes in my life, but some things have remained constant—like the tradition of Monday dinner with Clara and Rosalie.

With a quiet sigh, I lock the boutique's door, setting the stage for the next scene in my day.

Later, as I swing open the door to The Spotted Lily, the scent of strong spices and freshly baked goodies floods my senses. It's coming from the adjoining room that houses Queen of Tarts, and it is scrumptious.

The warm and cozy ambiance of our favorite local eatery never fails to envelop me like a comforting hug. The Spotted Lilly is the perfect spot to unwind and catch up with Rosalie and Clara after a long day. The murmur of chatter, the soft jazz playing in the background, and the comforting scents from the adjoining bakery create the perfect atmosphere to spill the beans about my ... date.

Rosie and Clara are going to be as shocked as I was the moment I noticed Mark in that bar.

My friends are already nestled comfortably in one of the worn leather couches, grinning like cats who've just discovered a bowl of cream. Clara practically bounces in her seat as I approach, her eyes sparkling with unbridled curiosity.

"Ella, over here! Spill the beans, lady! How was the date with your MindMate match?"

Rosie nods in agreement, her warm eyes glinting with intrigue over her steaming mug of tea.

"Hi, you two," I reply with a chuckle, sinking into the plush seat next to Clara. "Geez, you both act as though I've just returned from a covert spy mission. The date was ... nice."

"Nice?" Clara's nose wrinkles at the word. "Nice is how you describe a new haircut or a polite neighbor, not a date with a potential love interest. Especially now that you're fasting."

Rosie snickers, swirling her coffee. "She's got you there, Ella. Nice is a cop-out. We need juicy details."

And so, with their unwavering attention, I spill. I tell them about Wes, the nice guy aura, the polite conversation. But as I speak, I feel my heart clench at the knowledge that despite Wes' many admirable qualities, there just wasn't that spark. No fluttery feelings or stolen breaths. Nothing compared to ...

My narrative meanders towards Mark, my first love, now a soccer player for Nashville SC. I remind my friends about our summer of romance on Long Island, our serendipitous meeting at a Fuchsia 6 concert at Jones Beach, and the resulting whirlwind love affair. Although, it doesn't take much reminding. They remember well enough. As I delve into the story, my voice softens, the memories, sweet and bitter, flooding back.

There's a silence when I finish, our laughter and banter replaced by quiet contemplation.

"So, back then, he left," Clara finally speaks, her voice subdued. "Right? I mean, how could any of us forget how heartbroken you were?"

"Yeah," I confirm, my gaze lingering on the foam patterns of my chai latte.

"Well, it's okay," Rosie offers after a pause, her hand patting mine over the table. "This was just one night. And from what you've said, you're not missing much with Wes. I vote for putting all of it out of your mind and moving on."

Clara jumps in, the energy back in her tone. "She's right. You have time, Ella. Who knows? Maybe your love story is yet to unfold. Maybe it's closer than you think."

Before I can probe her cryptic comment, Rosie is standing up. Our table is ready for dinner. We rise too, eager to fill our bellies.

The waitress, a friendly blonde named Amber, ushers us towards our usual table at the back corner, where we get an unobstructed view of the restaurant and its attached bakery. The homey scent of yeast and warm dough, fused with the underlying sweetness of fresh-baked pastries, teases our senses, a familiar invitation to comfort and conversation.

We settle in, shrugging off our light cardigans despite the air conditioning humming in the background—a feeble attempt to combat the sticky summer evening. A lively chatter fills the restaurant, a hum of conversation blending with the occasional clink of silverware against porcelain.

Amber sets down a basket of warm, fluffy bread rolls nestled next to a dish of soft butter. Their familiar, inviting aroma wafts up to us. Rosie's eyes glint in anticipation, and she's quick to help herself, her love for bread a running joke among us. Clara and I follow suit, the warmth of the bread offering an immediate comfort.

"So, about Mark," Rosie says, fixing me with a no-nonsense stare, crumbs of bread caught in the corners of her mouth. "I get the idea you don't want to move on from running into him. Am I right?"

I feel my cheeks heating up, and Clara chimes in, "Yes, please, Ella. Do spill the tea. What are you thinking?"

The room fills with a faint echo of laughter from a table near the front, and the comforting hum of casual conversation punctuates my pause. I exhale a long breath and start, "Well, I met Mark during a summer on Long Island ..."

They already know, which makes the comment funny.

"Um hmm," Rosie says. "And now?"

"Isn't that the question of the day?" I ask with a smile.

As our dinner progresses, we share stories, laughter, a little bit of teasing, and an abundance of camaraderie. I divulge every bit of my unexpected run-in with Mark, the history they might or might not remember, the memories, and that undeniable chemistry that seems to have stood the test of time and distance. The confessions and reminiscences pave the way for more tales, more shared moments, more of us.

It's the binding thread of our friendship, this sharing and trust, and it fills me with a warm sense of belonging. As the evening wraps around us in a balmy embrace, we find ourselves pleasantly content.

This is the very stuff our Monday dinners are made of.

I've still got work to do back at the boutique, and it's inching closer to the time we'll have to say goodnight. But for now, we're here, we're together, and the world outside can wait. And while I'm caught between the past I can't forget and the present that's shaping up to be quite interesting, I feel incredibly grateful for the constants in my life—Rosie and Clara.

As we finish our dinner, our laughter still echoing in the corners of The Spotted Lily, I look forward to the next adventure we'll have to recount at our table, especially if it involves the unexpected Mark Dane in my present life.

Tomorrow promises to be a very interesting day.

CHAPTER 4

ELLA

The next day is a bright and sunny one at The Romantics headquarters. There's a tinge of anticipation in the air as I make my way to the meeting room on the second floor, my heels clicking against the newly installed hardwood floor.

Rosie has warned me that there's a surprise waiting, and knowing her, it's going to be something special.

The door to the meeting room opens before I even reach for the knob, revealing Becca's grinning face. "Good, you're here!" She exclaims, her deep-set green eyes sparkling with excitement. She ushers me inside.

"Surprise!" Rosie and Clara echo, popping out from behind a large table covered in sketches, fabric samples, and half-eaten croissants from Queen of Tarts. A gasp escapes my lips as I take in the spectacle.

"What's going on?" I ask, trying to catch my breath. There's an unusually mischievous glint in Rosie's eyes as she and Clara exchange a look. The table is covered in varying shades of blush and ivory, with swatches of silk and satin scattered in a charming, haphazard way.

"We're having a design party for your new collection!" Rosie exclaims, her hands gesturing to the array of fabrics, trims, and other decorative materials that they've rounded up.

My heart gives a little flutter at the sight. "Oh, wow, this is … this is amazing." I move to the table, touching the silky smooth fabric, the intricate lace trim, the shimmery organza.

"We thought it'd be fun to help you get started," Clara explains, pushing a tray of delicious pastries in my direction. "Plus, we needed an excuse to raid Cece's new bakery."

Becca, ever the practical assistant, hands me a sketchpad and pencil. "Don't forget, you have a meeting with the photographer later for the portfolio shoot."

"Right," I reply, snapping back to reality.

As a wedding dress designer, my life revolves around the endless cycle of design, fittings, production, and photoshoots.

"Let's get started then!" Clara chirps, and the design session officially begins. As we delve into the process of creating, there's a sense of harmony that only comes from working with people you know inside out. It's creative chaos at its finest, and I wouldn't have it any other way.

I take a deep breath, pressing the soft white fabric of the dress sample I'm currently working on between my fingers. The air is filled with the warm glow of overhead lamps, and the gentle hum of sewing machines in the background.

I can't help but notice how pretty it all is. And I love being surrounded by pretty things.

"Guys, I just … I can't seem to shake him off my mind. Mark, I mean." I admit, setting down the fabric and leaning back in my chair.

Clara pauses in her threading of a needle, looking at me with wide eyes and raised brows. "Mark Dane? You're still on about him?" Her eyebrows shoot up in surprise, the needle forgotten in her hand.

Rosie looks at me thoughtfully over the rim of her glasses. She's working on a floral arrangement for an upcoming wedding, her hands deftly putting together a mix of pastel roses and baby's breath. "I mean, it's understandable, Ella. He was your first love after all. And seeing him again after all these years … it's bound to stir up some old feelings."

"And you're meeting him for coffee at some point, right?" Clara asks, her surprise morphing into curiosity. "What are you hoping would happen?"

I shrug, picking at a stray thread on the dress. "I don't know, really. Catch up, maybe? It's been a long time."

Rosie's gaze softens, her fingers pausing in the midst of her arrangement. "Ella, sweetie, it's okay to admit you're a little … shaken up. Mark wasn't just a fling. He meant something to you. A lot."

"But what about Wes?" Clara, ever practical, interrupts before I can reply. "You seemed to be getting along quite well with him, especially when you two were chatting via the app. Maybe a second date is in order."

"Yeah, Wes is nice," I admit, "but there isn't that … spark. I mean, it's easy with him, comfortable even. But with Mark, it's different. There's just this … chemistry."

They listen and nod, but don't tell me what to do. I appreciate that. I'll figure it out on my own. Eventually.

I turn my attention back to my work once more. It's an excellent, worthy distraction. Has been for years.

By the time we wrap up the session, my hands are smudged with pencil and my mind is buzzing with ideas. "I can't wait to start on these designs," I say, leafing through my sketchpad filled with rough drawings and fabric samples. "They'll make great additions to the new line."

Becca flashes me a bright smile. "They're going to be beautiful, Ella. The brides will love them." Her faith in me warms my heart, giving me the confidence I need to tackle this new collection.

"Alright, team," I say, shutting my sketchbook. "Let's call it a wrap. I need to prepare for that photography session. Rosie, Clara, Becca, thank you for today. It means a lot. More than you know."

As I make my way out of the meeting room, an overwhelming sense of gratitude fills me. Working with my best friends, doing what I love—I wouldn't trade it for anything else. But as I step out into the sultry summer air, the encounter from the other night at the Nashville bar comes rushing back.

Mark Dane, my long-lost summer love, now in town playing for Nashville SC. What a small world. I might like to date a sexy soccer player. I'd never imagined that, but I am now. He always did have the best legs. Strong, toned, delicious muscular legs.

I shake my head, pushing the memories aside. Now's not the time for nostalgia, or for getting turned on. I have designs to make and dresses to create. That's exactly what I plan on doing.

The past can wait.

For now, I'm focused on tulle, satin, and yes, love. But not the kind that Mark Dane offers. The love I have for my job and my beautiful life.

The sun is still high in the sky, a few lazy clouds meandering their way across the bright blue expanse. Sonny Hoover and his film crew wave to me through the window of Rosie's flower shop as I step out of The Romantics building. They're still focused primarily on Rosalie's Flowers. I don't mind. I know my time will come.

My phone buzzes with a text from my mom. Patricia Lovelace checks in on me every now and then. We aren't close in the sense that I tell her intimate details of my life, but I appreciate her cheerful support. Dad's, too.

MOM: Hope you had a lovely day, honey. Love you.

Me: Love you too, Mom. Day's not over yet, off to a photoshoot.

. . .

I POCKET MY PHONE, my eyes meeting my assistant's across the sidewalk. The ever-efficient Becca has the organized hustle of a general commanding her troops, and today, she's leading our foray into the photoshoot for my new line of bridal gowns.

As we walk to my car parked down the street, I notice the calm that hangs over Loveland. The town is quaint and serene, its peaceful ambiance providing a stark contrast to the whirlwind of emotions I find myself tangled in. Even though my family is from New York, I grew up here, in small-town Tennessee. I cherish my Northern roots, but I wouldn't want to live anywhere else but here. It's the perfect place for me.

"Ella, are you ready for this?" Becca breaks through my reverie, her question nudging me back to the moment. She's waving the car keys in her hand, her brows arched in question.

Truth be told, the thought of Mark Dane and our upcoming coffee date vies for attention with the excitement over the photoshoot, leaving me in a state of flux. My stomach is performing gymnastics, but I keep my face composed. I can't let my jitters overshadow the importance of today. I'm not the only one who has worked hard for this. Becca deserves my best. I don't want her to worry that my attention is elsewhere.

"Absolutely," I respond, giving her a reassuring smile.

"Good," she replies, somewhat skeptically.

Oh, well. Off we go.

The ride to the photoshoot is relatively quiet, both of us lost in our own thoughts. As we pull up to the venue, a beautifully restored barn on the outskirts of Loveland, I feel a rush of pride. These dresses, this photoshoot … they represent my dreams. The fruits of my tireless work.

And yet, the thought of Mark manages to weave itself into this moment.

Of course, it does.

Mark, who was a part of my past, who's now stepped back into my present, his memory tinging my triumph with a touch of nostalgia.

Mark, Mark, Mark.

It feels like that's all I think about anymore. What's even happening to me?

We step out of the car, the late afternoon sun casting long shadows around us. I steal a glance at Becca, her face focused and determined. I draw strength from her, pushing the thoughts of my love life away for now.

"Let's do this, Becca," I say, my voice steady, my resolve strong. We have a photoshoot to ace, dreams to turn into reality. My love life can wait. It will have to.

With a deep breath, I walk towards the barn, my heels clicking against the gravel, my mind filled with the anticipation of what's to come. The day is yet young, the sun far from setting, and there's work to be done. And right now, that's all that matters.

When my work is finished, I'll let myself think about Mark. About Wes. About my tangled heart. But right now, I'm Ella Lovelace, bridal boutique owner, and I have a photoshoot to conquer.

CHAPTER 5

MARK

$\mathcal{J}$ ust as the team's chatter begins to fade into the background, the blaring whistle of Coach Henderson brings me back to the present. I turn around to see his sharp eyes darting across the field, corralling his soccer players as he waves us over for the end-of-practice huddle.

"Good work today, team. Remember, practice doesn't make perfect. Perfect practice makes perfect," Coach Henderson's voice echoes around us, his favored mantra falling flat in the thick, humid Nashville air. As he starts to discuss our strategy for the upcoming match, my mind begins to drift off again.

There's a pull in my gut, a nagging feeling that's been with me since two nights ago. It's a combination of nostalgia, regret, and something else I can't quite put my finger on.

It's been nearly a decade, but Ella's face is as clear in my mind now as it was all those years ago.

Our reunion wasn't exactly the fairy tale scenario I

had imagined in my idle moments. The memories from that night are a blur—her shocked expression, the soft edges of her eyes, the way her lips moved when she said my name—but there's one thing that remains crystal clear. Ella Lovelace, the girl I fell in love with one unforgettable summer, is just as captivating now as she was back then.

"Dane!" My attention is jerked back to the present as I hear my name called. Coach Henderson is done with his speech and is now sending us off. I nod and force a grin, slapping my teammates on the back as we disperse.

I'm the last one to leave the field, the setting sun casting long shadows over the empty stands. Soccer, the one constant in my life that's always provided solace, now feels like an afterthought. Ella has consumed my thoughts, and I know I can't ignore these feelings.

Ella was my world, back then. Our summer together on Long Island was glorious. Not to mention, sensual and exhilarating. She opened my eyes to an existence that was like nothing I'd ever known before, and like nothing I've found since. We were like two parts of one whole. Two hearts that were made for each other. That's not me exaggerating or being dramatic. I kid you not. She and I were something special.

I've never gotten over her. I don't think I ever could. I never should have let her go. Breaking up with Ella was the single biggest mistake of my life.

I'm not ashamed to admit that Ella was on my mind when I took this job in Nashville. If we could somehow find our way back to each other again, it would mean everything to me. It would make my life complete.

No joke.

As I head to my car, gym bag over one shoulder, I pull out my phone. I find her number, a digit sequence I'd committed to memory all those years ago. Before I can second-guess myself, I press call.

Here goes nothing.

It rings a few times before going to voicemail. The sound of her recorded voice sends a jolt of electricity through me. She sounds just like the Ella I remember.

Her voice is enchanting to me. Almost like a siren's call. But in a good way. If that makes sense. It probably doesn't.

"Hey, it's Ella. Sorry I can't take your call right now. Leave a message and I'll get back to you as soon as I can."

I hesitate for a moment, then leave a message. "Hey Ella, it's Mark. I was thinking about our conversation the other night, and I was wondering if you'd like to get that coffee sometime soon. Call me back when you get a chance."

As I hang up, I feel good. The ball is in her court now. She's busy building her bridal boutique, and I'm here, in the groove of my career as a professional athlete.. We're miles apart in terms of our life paths, but there's still that one common thread that binds us together—our past.

Tonight, under the evening stars, I make a silent vow to myself. No matter what happens next, I won't let Ella slip away this time. I can't afford to live with that kind of regret. That woman is a chapter in my life that has remained open for too long. It's high time to find out if that chapter has a happy ending or if it's time to turn the page.

One way or another, I'm taking action. Taking the shot. I just have to come up with a game plan. That shouldn't be too hard. I'll figure something out.

As the last rays of the sun dip below the horizon, I feel hopeful. The past may be a complicated maze, but the future looks like a promising journey. It's time to delve into the past, one memory at a time, to see where it leads.

I drive off into the Nashville night knowing one thing for sure—this is only the beginning.

CHAPTER 6

MARK

The next day, the buzz of my phone interrupts the monotony of the Nashville traffic, and I sneak a quick glance at the screen. A message from Ella. My heart beats a bit faster. I swipe it open and see a video attachment.

"Can't believe I'm sending you this," her text reads, "But Becca insisted you should see it."

I'm parked now, curiosity piqued. I tap the play button.

The video is a behind-the-scenes look at a photoshoot that happened yesterday, filled with models adorned in gorgeous, lace-and-silk gowns. My eyes are drawn to one figure, not in front of the camera, but behind it. *Ella.* Even in the low resolution of the video, her sparkle is unmistakable. She looks beautiful. Radiant, even. She's directing the models, her movements graceful and assured. She's in her element, and a wave of pride swells in me. Her designs, her vision ... all coming to life right before my eyes.

That's my girl.

For a moment, I allow myself to get lost in the sight of her, the very picture of elegance and determination. My thumb slides across the screen, pausing the video to capture the moment when she throws her head back in laughter, caught in the joy of her creation. In that second, it hits me just how much I've missed her.

Ella Lovelace, the woman who had once been more important to me than anything else. More than the sun, the moon, and all the stars. It might sound sappy, but it's true.

"Damn," I mutter under my breath, the reality of the situation sinking in.

That part of our lives was over now. We were both on different paths, yet a part of me still yearned for her. The sight of Ella looking so content, so fulfilled ... It stirred up a mix of emotions I wasn't prepared for.

"Mark, are you there?" My best friend, and fellow Nashville SC teammate, Toby Barnes interrupts my thoughts through the car's speakerphone. I completely forgot I'd been talking to him.

I clear my throat, hitting the end button on the video and switch back to the call. "Yeah, man. Just got a bit distracted. What's up?"

"Training starts in half an hour, dude. Don't tell me you're still at home."

"Almost there," I lie, even though I'm still parked, stuck in a daydream, with Ella's laughter still echoing in my ears. I restart the car, shifting gears as I shake off the last remnants of my thoughts.

There's a beep as a new message comes in. Ella

again. I open it, heart pounding, only to see a short text. "Good luck with training."

I smile, even though a part of me aches with the simplicity of it. We used to be so much more than this. But for now, I'll take what I can get. I quickly type back a "Thanks, Ella" before putting my phone away and joining the flow of traffic.

My thoughts are still with the woman who's managing to keep me distracted amidst the whirl of chiffon and satin. And maybe, just maybe, it's not only the traffic that's keeping my heart racing.

Of course, it isn't the traffic.

"Pull it together, Mark Dane," I mutter to myself. It's easier said than done when Ella Lovelace is involved.

As the cityscape whizzes past my window, my mind is already planning our upcoming coffee meet. It's been a while since we've had a proper catch-up, and the prospect sends a thrill down my spine. Maybe this is the start of something new, or perhaps a revisitation of something old. Either way, I'm here for it.

For now, though, I have to focus on the road and the upcoming training. Soccer first, then Ella. Life's full of priorities, and I've got to take them one at a time.

The image of Ella at her photoshoot fades as I pass the Fairgrounds and the Nashville SC training ground comes into view, but something tells me it's not going to be that easy to forget.

I can't help but blink at the onslaught of memories that come barreling into my mind at the thought of that summer, the one Ella and I spent together on Long

Island. *Damn.* That summer was everything—the sun, the beach, the music—it was all Ella.

The world spun on its axis because of Ella.

When I arrive and join my teammates in the training room, I find myself distracted again.

"Hey, Mark," Toby's voice snaps me back to reality. I shake my head, trying to clear the lingering haze of Ella-induced nostalgia.

"Yeah, mate?" I reply, glancing over at him. His face is lit up by the glow of his laptop screen, which is filled with more stats and figures than I care to decipher.

"I've got a charity event coming up. Vanderbilt Children's Hospital. They're hosting a soccer clinic. We're all expected to show up. It's not optional."

"Great," I murmur, only half-listening.

I let my mind wander back to that summer. My brain, it seems, has a mind of its own and it's hell-bent on reliving those precious memories. It's a slideshow of beachside barbecues, shared laughter, secret kisses stolen under the moonlight, and heart-to-heart talks that lasted until dawn. The image of Ella, in her sundress with flowers in her blonde hair, laughing with the sun setting behind her, still sends a jolt through me.

"Mark, are you even listening?" Toby's exasperated voice jolts me from my daydream.

"Yeah," I say, tearing my thoughts from Ella to look at Toby. "Charity event. Got it."

In truth, I love these events, getting to teach the kids, seeing their faces light up with joy when they kick a goal. It reminds me of why I started playing soccer in the first place. Yet, today, my mind seems to be running a marathon back to Long Island, the finish line being the start of a love story that ended too soon.

I remember our last night there, some random concert at Jones Beach.

We were young, barely out of our teens, fuelled by the euphoria of our love and the adrenaline of the music. I recall the taste of cheap beer on her lips as I kissed her, the neon lights from the stage reflecting in her eyes, the way her body moved against mine.

The phone call comes in the middle of this vivid recollection, and my heart nearly jumps out of my chest at the sharp ring. Toby's amused smirk tells me he knows exactly where my mind was.

"You planning on answering that, Romeo?" he teases, pushing the phone towards me.

With a glare in his direction, I pick up the phone, clearing my throat. "Mark Dane speaking."

"Hey, Mark. It's Ella again. Ella Lovelace." Her voice sounds just like I remember, soft, sweet, like the first warm day of spring.

My heart trips over itself.

"Um, you don't have to say your last name," I reply with a chuckle.

"Okay."

She talks more about the photoshoot, her new bridal line, and the professional photographer. I can hear the excitement in her voice, and it's infectious. Ella's always been like that. Her energy and enthusiasm are powerful. It's hard not to get swept up.

As the call ends, I'm left with the echo of her voice in

my ears and the certain resurgence of feelings that I thought I'd buried deep.

Ella Lovelace. The girl who captured my heart in a summer, only to disappear with the setting sun.

Yet, here she is, back in my life. My mind knows better. It warns me to tread lightly, and not to fall down that rabbit hole again. But my heart, damn my stupid heart, it's already halfway down, chasing after the memories of sun-kissed skin and laughter-filled nights.

Ella Lovelace is back, and I have a feeling that my world, once again, is about to spin off its axis.

I stare at the phone long after I've hung up, my mind full to the brim with thoughts, memories, and unanswered questions.

The room is silent except for the soft clicking of Toby's keyboard. I narrow my eyes and wonder what the coming days will bring. I wonder how much they'll look like those long-lost summer days in New York, and whether Ella and I can ever recapture what we once had.

The answer is as unknown as the outcome of the next soccer match, and it fills me with an anticipation I haven't felt in a long time. I can't wait to find out.

I draw in a deep breath, squaring my shoulders. No matter what the future holds, one thing is certain—it's going to be one hell of a ride.

It's game on, Ella Lovelace. Game on.

CHAPTER 7

ELLA

In the sleepy stillness of the morning, I blink my eyes open. My alarm clock reads 6:30 am, the digital numerals glowing an unfriendly red. My room is lit with a soft glow from the rising sun, the curtains letting through just enough light to encourage my wakefulness.

I have a lot on my mind.

The photoshoot. The new bridal line. Mark. Nashville. Mark. Mark.

Did I mention Mark?

As much as I want to roll over and slip back into the safety of sleep, there's *too much* on my mind. I groan and sit up, pushing my unruly hair out of my face. I glance at my phone sitting on the bedside table, half-expecting, half-hoping for a message from Mark.

Nothing. I give myself a mental shake.

I can't be doing this to myself.

I get up, deciding that a hot shower will help wake me and clear my head. As I stand under the hot spray, my thoughts still drift back to Mark. The past has a strange way of catching up when you least expect it.

As the water cascades over me, I let myself remember the summer we shared on Long Island. Long walks on the beach, concerts under the stars, Mark's laugh echoing in the still night air.

The water mixes with the tears I hadn't realized I'd shed.

"Get a grip, Ella," I murmur to myself, rubbing the water off my face. As I step out of the shower, I wrap myself in my soft, terrycloth robe and walk back to my bedroom.

I look at the design sketches I left spread out on my worktable last night. Delicate pencil lines capture the silhouettes of ethereal gowns and sophisticated veils. I've put so much of myself into this bridal line. I let my fingers trace the pencil strokes, feeling the dream take a tangible form under my touch.

Breakfast is a simple affair—yogurt and fresh fruits with a hot cup of coffee. I sit by the kitchen window, letting the morning light spill over me, the sounds of our small town slowly rising with the sun.

Despite my tumultuous thoughts, there's a sense of peace that accompanies the morning. A new day, a fresh start.

I sigh, leaving my dishes in the sink and heading back to my bedroom. There's work to be done. I'm working from home this morning, and I need to finalize the designs for the catalog. The printers are waiting.

I glance once again at my silent phone, then shake my head.

No more distractions.

As I begin to gather my sketchpads and colored pencils, I remind myself of the job at hand. The bridal line has been a dream come true, and I can't let personal emotions cloud my professional judgment.

I sit down, the pencils feeling familiar and comforting in my hand.

I lose myself in the rhythm of work, each stroke of the pencil, each line and curve helping to push Mark Dane's handsome face to the back of my mind. By the time my phone rings, I'm lost in a world of organza, tulle, and lace. I startle, the pencil slipping from my hand and landing on the sketch in progress.

With a sigh, I pick up the phone. Becca's name flashes on the screen. I slide to answer, holding the phone between my shoulder and ear as I retrieve the fallen pencil.

"Hey, Becca," I say, trying to keep my voice light. After all, the day is still young and there's a lot to do.

"Hey, Ella. You ready for today?" Her voice, chirpy and upbeat, is a balm to my chaotic morning. I smile, a small part of my anxiety easing.

"Ready as I'll ever be," I reply, a newfound determination setting in.

Let the day bring what it may, I have gowns to design and a dream to realize. The printers are waiting to document my designs in a format that can be distributed to bridal shops far and wide.

The phone call with Becca ends on a positive note, and I'm left looking at the mess of sketches and fabrics scattered over the worktable. A mess that reminds me what a beautiful life I've created for myself.

Life goes on. With or without Mark Dane.

As soon as I step foot inside the Romantics' building, I am embraced by a chaos that feels like coming home. The spacious floor in the common entryway area is buzzing with energy—every corner humming with laughter and camaraderie, along with the occasional shriek of a near catastrophe. The air is fragrant with a blend of fresh fabric, hot coffee, and the faint metallic tang of the old industrial building.

I'm immediately greeted by Rosie, whose already radiant face brightens even more when she sees me. Her waves bounce like pretty springs as she skips towards me, arms extended. "Ella!" she exclaims, wrapping me in a bear hug. Clara follows suit, her warm hug just as welcoming.

"Ladies," I greet them, "it's one hot mess in here." I sweep an arm around to indicate the surrounding disorder.

"That's the best kind of mess," Clara winks at me, her eyes twinkling. Rosie bursts into giggles, the infectious sound echoing through the room and sparking a round of laughter among everyone within hearing distance. The Romantics, we are a family—an unusually loud and dramatic one—but family, nonetheless.

I drop my bag onto a nearby table and get straight to work. I have to finalize the designs for the catalog that's soon to be printed. It's a riot of fabrics, colors, and notes spread across the wooden tabletop, each design a testament to hours of painstaking work and the relentless pursuit of perfection.

As I sift through the sketches, my fingers brushing lightly over the crisp paper, my mind flashes back to the beach on Long Island, the waves crashing, the scent of the sea mingling with Mark's cologne. I shake my head, trying to dislodge the memory. This is neither the time nor place to dwell on what-ifs and could-have-beens.

Frankly, it's getting ridiculous. I don't think I've ever obsessed about a man the way I have been over the past few days. Well, other than that one summer.

Sheesh.

"Thinking about the new heartthrob in town?" Clara's voice jolts me back to reality. I shoot her a look. She has a knack for catching me at my most vulnerable moments.

"Who? Mark Dane?" I feign indifference, but a heat rises to my cheeks. "That nobody?"

My joke lands flat. My friends are well aware of the butterflies-in-stomach feeling I've been having since my run-in with Mark.

Clara raises an eyebrow, and Rosie, the ever-helpful one, adds, "He is really cute, though. And you two were a hot item, back in the day. Have you set a time for that coffee date yet?"

I roll my eyes, "No. I don't know. Can we focus on work, please?"

They agree, reluctantly, knowing full well we'll circle back to the topic soon enough.

The rest of the day is a whirl of colors, fabrics, and

incessant chatter. By the end of it, I feel like a wrung-out washcloth, but there's a peculiar sense of satisfaction in seeing my latest design portfolio taking shape. As I stare at the sketches spread out on the table, my heart brims with pride and a touch of fear. It's terrifying and exhilarating in equal measures, pouring my heart and soul into these designs, then putting them out for the world to judge.

"I hope people like these designs," I say, mostly to myself.

"Oh, they will," Rosie says as she gives my hand a squeeze. "They're superb, Ella. Truly. You've outdone yourself this time."

Clara nods her agreement.

As I stand there, in the heart of our bustling building, surrounded by friends who long ago turned into family, my heart aches for another pair of eyes. Eyes that held pride and admiration whenever they looked at my work. Eyes that belong to a certain professional soccer player who's been invading my thoughts lately.

I swallow hard, forcing the memories down.

I'm still working away as the night falls, painting the sky with a riot of colors.

Through the tall factory windows, I watch as the orange and pink hues blend into a soft, velvety darkness, the transitioning skyline reflecting the whirlwind of emotions churning within me. As the day ends, I find myself yearning for something more, something beyond the familiar confines of this old factory building.

Or maybe, just maybe, I'm yearning for *someone*.

Later, at home, I'm standing in the corner of my walk-in closet, clutching the phone in my sweaty palm, my heart pounding like a teenager who's just been asked out on a first date. My stomach flips as I hear Mark's voice on the other end of the line, his tone easy and calm as if we're talking about the weather.

"Hey, Ella. It's Mark. Just wanted to see if you'd be free to grab that coffee tomorrow?"

There's a moment of silence that stretches into an eternity, my mind spinning like a hamster on a wheel. Finally, I manage to stutter out a response, "Sure, Mark. That sounds great."

There's a soft chuckle on his end, "Great. Let's say noon at The Grind?"

The Grind is in Loveland. That means he's willing to make the thirty minute drive down from Nashville to see me. I'm not sure he's ever been to Loveland.

I swallow the lump in my throat, trying to sound nonchalant, "Yeah, sure. See you then."

"Ella?" he asks.

"Yeah?"

"I'm looking forward to it," he says in that smooth baritone of his.

It makes me wet with desire, just hearing Mark's voice. I'm not sure it even matters what he's saying. My body remembers what a talented lover he is.

"Me, too," I manage.

The call ends, but my heart continues its erratic rhythm.

I sink down onto the plush carpet of my closet, my mind reeling with the sudden realization. I'm going on a date with Mark Dane. *The* Mark Dane. *My* Mark Dane.

Memories flood back in waves. Long summer nights

filled with laughter and whispered confessions under the starlit sky. Sun-kissed skin and tangled limbs on the sandy beaches of Long Island. Warm, lazy afternoons spent lying in the shade of towering oaks, his head in my lap as I traced the features of his face, committing them to memory.

That was a different time. A different us. A lot has changed.

But, has it really? Could we pick up where we left off, as if those eight years apart never happened? Or am I setting myself up for heartbreak once again?

Dammit. I'm not sure.

I shake off the flurry of doubts and worries threatening to engulf me and push myself off the floor. I can't afford to get lost in my thoughts right now. I have a date to prepare for. A date with Mark.

I step out of my closet and move toward my ensuite bathroom. Looking at my reflection in the mirror, I see a woman on the brink of something new. Something thrilling, yet terrifying. Something that could change everything. A soft blush rises in my cheeks at the thought of seeing Mark again.

Mark Dane. Professional soccer player. The same Mark who left all those years ago, leaving a shattered heart in his wake.

The same Mark who I was about to see again. Tomorrow. At noon.

Although, granted, maybe I need a dose of reality. Can I trust my judgment right now?

Back then—when he was mine—Mark was shy. He wasn't ambitious. At least, I didn't think so. I had serious doubts about whether he could keep up with me.

Am I building him up in my mind now? Is the inflated memory of the guy better than the actual guy?

I let out a shaky laugh.

I don't know. *Hell.*

The universe certainly has a sense of humor.

As I prepare for bed and feed Gonzo, my mind is a whirlwind of thoughts and emotions. There's excitement, anticipation, a touch of anxiety, and a whole lot of nostalgia.

Tomorrow is a big day. Bigger than I'd imagined.

I sink into my plush pillows, the soft fabric against my skin offering little comfort. Sleep seems like a distant dream, but I force my eyes shut, willing myself to relax. Tomorrow, I'll face whatever comes my way.

Tonight, I need rest. Because tomorrow, I'm going on a date with Mark Dane.

And, I'm equal parts excited and terrified. But, isn't that what makes life interesting?

Smiling at the thought, I finally let myself drift into sleep, dreams of sandy beaches and soccer fields filling my mind.

Tomorrow is going to be one hell of a day.

CHAPTER 8

MARK

The Nashville heat is already clinging to my skin as I leave the charity event at Vanderbilt Children's Hospital. Playing pro soccer for Nashville SC, I'm used to exertion. Not to mention, the adrenaline and the all-consuming energy of the sport. But recently, in quieter moments, a different kind of fervor tugs at me. It's nostalgia for my past with Ella Lovelace.

I slide into the leather seat of my car, feeling the cool AC breathing life back into me, when my phone buzzes. It's a text from Ella. My heart does a familiar somersault, the way it does when I'm about to score a goal.

"See you at The Grind at noon. Don't be late, Dane."

A grin tugs at the corners of my mouth, evoking memories of her scolding me during our summer in Long Island for my chronic tardiness. Back then, we were just two kids, basking in the glow of young love. Now, those moments live as echoes, filling the silent crevices of my heart with a gentle warmth.

Our impending meeting leaves me with a blend of excitement and apprehension.

Today isn't just about Ella and me, it's about being under a spotlight. Sonny Hoover, along with his crew, including Clara's fiancé Sean O'Shea, are filming for a docu-series featuring The Romantics. It's a big deal that Ella wants me to be on camera.

I hope it means that she sees me being a part of her future. Otherwise, she'd keep me tucked away, right?

As the cityscape of Nashville unfurls around me, my mind drifts back to Ella. Our history is a tapestry of intense emotions, filled with color and vivacity, much like Ella herself. Memories of her shimmering laughter, our arguments sparking with passion, and the over-whelming sense of belonging I felt with her flood my thoughts.

Sure, we can't return to the carefree, sun-kissed days of our youth. We've grown, changed, and shaped our separate lives. But there's a part of me, however small, that hopes we might rekindle the friendship we once shared.

Friendship. Yeah, who am I kidding? I want much more. Friendship is a good start.

As Nashville's city lights give way to the more subdued scenery of Loveland, my excitement mounts. I'm not just traversing the thirty-minute stretch of highway separating the two towns. I'm crossing a bridge of memories in my mind, and hopefully, rebuilding one that had been left in ruins.

Parking outside The Grind, the quaint charm of the small-town coffee shop invokes a rush of anticipation and wistfulness. It reminds me of the coffee shops on Long Island.

I glance at my dashboard clock—11:45 AM. "I've actually managed to be early," I muse, shaking my head in disbelief. I rake my hand through my hair and square my shoulders.

Bracing myself for the onslaught of emotions seeing Ella will inevitably bring, I exit the car. A part of me also expects the arrival of Sonny's crew, capturing this real, unscripted reunion. I suppose this footage will offer a different facet to the glamorous world of The Romantics. I suppose it doesn't matter, as long as Ella is happy having me take part.

"Here's to old times and new beginnings," I murmur to myself, turning my gaze to the coffee shop. And with that, I stride towards what I hope marks the start of a renewed chapter in our interconnected story.

Since it's almost high noon in Loveland, the humidity is building up. Summer heat hangs heavy in the air, sticking to the skin like a second layer. I take a deep breath, relishing the potent scent of coffee that dances around me as I step into The Grind.

The cafe isn't what I expected. The place is cool and dim, an old gas station converted into a modern blend of comfort and industrial design. The aroma of freshly ground coffee, the low hum of conversations, the soft jazz playing overhead—all of it combines to form an ambiance that feels both homey and exotic at once.

The place is teeming with people, but it's her I spot right away.

There she is, vibrant as the summer day, talking

animatedly with the barista, Hope Gallagher, a petite woman with a warm smile. I recognize Hope because Ella told me about her. She often mans a coffee cart in The Romantics building.

Ella's golden waves cascade down her shoulders, shimmering under the dim lights. The way she moves is fluid, like water following the path of least resistance. I watch as she tilts her head back, releasing a laugh that rings clear and bright over the murmur of the room. It's a sound that does funny things to my chest.

But it's not just the laughter. It's her entire presence. There's a fire to Ella, something magnetic that draws your gaze and holds it. I've never met anyone quite like her before—someone who could make leather and lace look like they were always meant to be together.

She's clad in one of her usual ensembles: a leather jacket thrown over a soft lace dress. Her red boots, sleek and polished, contrast against the feminine cut of her clothes. But that's Ella. A living paradox, equal parts soft and hard, tough and delicate. She's a woman who owns a bridal boutique and yet has a fondness for reptiles, a woman who finds pleasure in using hilariously creative names for anatomy, a woman who rides motorcycles and bungees off bridges.

She excites me, in more ways than one.

I feel almost nervous as I approach her, a buzzing excitement that I try to mask beneath a calm exterior. I'm usually good at keeping my feelings hidden.

The door behind me swings open again, pulling me out of my daze. I glance over my shoulder to find Sonny Hoover, Sean O'Shea, and the rest of the camera crew trailing in. Ella told me about them, too. I recognize them based on her descriptions.

There's no escaping the reality that I'm here under the spotlight—on camera and being documented. I stifle a sigh, reminding myself that I signed up for this, even though at this moment, it feels like a necessary evil to endure.

Sonny catches my eye, then gives me a nod. He's a seasoned professional, this guy, with an aura of calm that belies the chaos that probably ensues in his wake. As I watch, he takes in the layout of the cafe with a practiced eye, instantly transforming from laid-back old guy to commanding director.

Looking at the camera crew, my nerves threaten to get the best of me. Until now, the documentary filming felt distant and abstract. But now it's real. It's tangible. And I'm right in the middle of it, with no script to follow. But then, life doesn't come with a script. Does it?

Give 'em your best, Dane.

Squaring my shoulders, I draw a deep breath, readying myself for whatever comes next. Today isn't about the cameras or the filming. It's about getting reacquainted with Ella and understanding more about the enigma that she is.

I begin to walk towards her, the sound of my boots on the concrete floor punctuating the moment. There's no turning back now. But then again, I don't want to. I'm on a path that's new and exciting, and it leads straight to a woman who could be a perfect chapter in my life's book—one that I'm eager to write.

As I draw closer to Ella, I grin like a man who is

smitten. I'm about to dive headfirst into an adventure with my old love. Somehow, I have a feeling it's going to be one hell of a ride.

CHAPTER 9

ELLA

"Mark Dane," I tease as we sit across the tiny round table from each other at The Grind. We have a cozy spot by the window with a view of the streetscape outside. We've enjoyed our coffee and lunch and are ready for whatever's next. I raise my eyebrow at his sudden enthusiasm for pastries, "If I didn't know better, I'd say you're nervous." Mark, however, shoots me a sideways smile, unashamed. It's both infuriating and endearing in equal parts.

"This place just makes really good lemon bars, Ella," he defends himself, already looking around for the plate with more. "Sue me."

I laugh, glancing at the cameras that are pointed in our direction. I'm sure this scene will make for good footage. Sonny is surely pleased.

"I'll agree with you there," I say. "Cece Baker is the talent behind Queen of Tarts. She's new in town, but her baked goods are already legendary in these parts. Her bakery is in a small space that adjoins a local cafe called The Spotted Lily. Many local establishments are now selling her goods. Customers can't seem to get enough."

"I get it," he says. "Delicious."

I study him for a moment, appraising the man he's become.

He has the sexiest broad shoulders, a focused gaze, and a smirk that could drop any warm-blooded woman in her tracks. I remember the boy, the one with too-long hair and too-loud laughter, and I wonder what it'd be like to know the man. To learn his quirks and decipher the meaning behind his smiles. An entire world awaits me there, behind those familiar yet unfamiliar blue eyes, and the thought is as terrifying as it is thrilling.

I rode my motorcycle here, and I intend to take Mark for a little ride. I gesture at it through the window. He nods, letting me know that he's game.

"Let's get you on that bike before you consume their entire stock," I suggest, eyeing the old motorbike parked by the curb. The '67 Triumph Bonneville is my pride and joy, a nod to simpler times when all I wanted was the open road and Mark Dane riding pillion. Today, the roles are reversed. The road seems a little more intimidating, and Mark Dane? He's going to be the one in the driver's seat.

"You're going to ride in all that lace?" he asks, already knowing the answer to the question.

"Never stopped me before."

We both chuckle. Mark knows I'm no wallflower. He's always appreciated my ... wild side. I used to think he couldn't match me, though, and that I'd overpower and overwhelm him. I'm curious to see whether I was right.

The afternoon sun casts shadows across the pavement as Mark confidently straddles the bike, his legs a perfect fit on either side. I recall the countless times I had him on the back of my bike, clinging onto me as we sped down the winding oceanside roads on Long Island. His warm body against mine, the feel of his arms wrapped around my waist—these were memories etched into the very fabric of my being.

The bike I had back then wasn't nearly as nice. It was more of a scooter, really. My parents bought me this one as a gift for my college graduation.

"Helmet on," I instruct, more to distract myself from the sudden onslaught of nostalgia. He obliges, adjusting the strap beneath his chiseled jawline. I remind myself to breathe.

"Ready?" he asks. The word is muffled through the helmet, but the anticipation is clear in his gaze.

I swallow, taking a moment to reassure myself. This is just Mark Dane. The same boy who fell off a bike twice when he tried to impress me, the same boy who's seen me in my best and worst, the same boy who

...

The shrill ring of my phone slices through my thoughts like a hot knife through butter. I blink, looking down at the screen. It's Patrick, Rosie's fiancé and an architect working on the renovations at our building. He hardly calls, unless it's urgent. Especially during the day.

"I need to take this," I tell Mark, watching as his eyebrows pull together in a slight frown.

Ignoring the sinking feeling in my stomach, I answer the call.

The next few minutes are a blur. Patrick's frantic voice echoes in my ears, throwing words like "renovations," "delay," and "unexpected complications" at me. The Romantics building, our safe haven, our pride and joy, has run into some unforeseen issues. Renovations were supposed to breathe new life into the place. But right now, it feels like it's teetering on the brink of disaster.

I squeeze my eyes shut, pressing the phone closer to my ear as if the physical contact could somehow resolve the issue at hand. My mind races, trying to process the information, trying to devise a plan of action. Everything fades into the background—the motorcycle ride with Mark, our conversation—becoming a distant echo against the urgency of Patrick's voice.

"I need you here, Ella. We can't move forward until you approve the new changes. I wouldn't have called if it wasn't absolutely necessary."

I know he wouldn't. Patrick's as reliable as they come, and the fact that he's calling for help? It sends a shiver of worry down my spine. "Alright, Patrick, I'm coming back to the office. I'll be there shortly."

Ending the call, I glance at Mark. His helmet is off, and he's watching me with a concern that feels too heavy for the moment. My heart sinks as I take a deep breath, preparing myself for what comes next.

"Mark, I ... I have to go," I tell him, hating the disappointment that flashes across his face. "There's a problem with the renovations on our building, and they need me there."

He nods, understanding dawning in his eyes, even if it's laced with a hint of disappointment. He gets it. He knows what The Romantics means to me, what it represents. It's my dream, my heart, and my soul tied up in a bundle of tulle, satin, and lace. It's a part of me, and right now, that part is in trouble.

"It's okay, Ella. We can do this another day," he assures me, his disappointment hidden behind a mask of understanding. I let out a breath, nodding in gratitude. He throws me a small smile, reassuring in its own way.

"I'm sorry," I mumble.

"No need to be. We have time."

He's right, but that doesn't make it feel any better. It feels like Mark and I should sort things out as soon as possible. It feels like our reconciliation is already way overdue. As I ready my motorcycle for a solo trip, leaving behind the promise of an exciting afternoon, I can't help but wonder about the might-have-beens.

We say our goodbyes, and I promise to make this up to him.

The streets of Loveland are bathed in the golden hues of the summer sun as I weave through the light traffic. The quaint storefronts and tree-lined pavements are streaked with elongated shadows, and the day's energy is beginning to recede into a languid calm. But inside me, it's a whirlwind of thoughts. An echoing anxiety that refuses to settle.

Patrick's words keep replaying in my mind. They dance around, taunting my brain and squeezing my heart. I try to soothe myself, reminding my heart to maintain a steady rhythm, reminding my mind that we have faced challenges before and overcome them. But it doesn't help much.

As I reach The Romantics' building, I find Patrick pacing outside. He's on the phone, gesturing frantically. The sight of him, usually so composed, looking so frazzled sends a chill down my spine. I park the bike and approach him, trying to steady my shaky hands.

"Patrick?" I call out, alerting him to my presence.

I need things to be okay. I'm taking a risk in seeing Mark again. I'm not sure I can take much additional stress on top of that.

Patrick ends his call and turns to me, a sigh of relief escaping him. We head inside the building to meet up with Rosie and Clara, with Patrick explaining the details of the issue. Apparently, some structural flaws had been discovered that could potentially compromise the safety of the building. It's a mess, and one that needs immediate attention. If we can't correct things, and quickly, the building will have to be evacuated and shuttered.

As we walk around the building, assessing the extent of the damage, a part of me wants to crumble and give in to the disappointment. But I push it away, focusing on the task at hand. I can't afford to break down. Not when The Romantics—and my life's work—hangs in the balance.

Hours blur into each other as we scramble to find

solutions, to make plans and schedules, to turn this setback into an opportunity. Patrick is a rock, keeping us grounded even as I find myself teetering on the edge of panic. His calm and his faith in our ability to turn things around soothes my frazzled nerves.

As the evening seeps in, casting long shadows, I find myself standing in what was to be the new bridal suite. The room is half-finished, a stark reminder of our halted progress. I'm alone, Patrick having left to handle another crisis and my friends having retreated to their respective offices. The sounds of the town have faded to a distant murmur, the building is quiet, and the weight of the situation finally hits me.

I lean against a wall, sliding down until I'm sitting on the cold concrete floor. My eyes roam the room, taking in the chaos and the uncertainty. I blink back tears, willing myself to stay strong.

And then my mind wanders to Mark. To the excitement in his eyes when he saw my motorcycle, to the laughter that warmed my heart, and to the conversation that stirred up old memories. I remember his understanding when I had to leave, his reassuring words, and his promise that there will be another day.

It's a strange comfort, a balm to my weary soul.

Suddenly, the day doesn't seem so dark. Yes, there's a problem. A big one. But there's also a solution waiting to be found, a team willing to work hard, and a ... friend ... who believes in me.

Right now, that's all I need.

As I rise from the floor, dusting myself off, a fresh determination fills me.

My friends and I will face this challenge head-on, just like we always have. And we will come out stronger, just like we always do.

I leave the building, the night wrapping around me like a comforting shroud. As I drive home on my motorcycle, the promise of a new day, a fresh start, and a chance to set things right fill me with hope. Tomorrow, we begin again.

Also tomorrow, I will make it up to Mark. The ride that we didn't have, the afternoon that was cut short ... I owe him that, and much more. As the evening light bathes the quiet streets of Loveland, I find myself smiling. After all, tomorrow is another day. Another chance. A chance to fix The Romantics building, and a chance to explore the new, more mature bond that's quietly taking shape between Mark and me.

The day might have ended on a tough note, but tomorrow, I resolve, will be a better one. And with that hopeful thought, I steer my bike towards home.

CHAPTER 10

MARK

The tension of the last 24 hours is seeping away, ebbing with the low hum of my Audi's engine as I rotate the wrench, securing my new Tennessee license plate to the back of the vehicle. I've lived here a few months now, and I'm finally feeling like an official Nashvillian.

Ella's world of chaos, the crisis at the Romantics building, her hurried departure—they're phantoms, shadows that lose their grip under the nurturing influence of the midday sun. With every tightened bolt, every polished piece of chrome, the serenity of routine replaces the echoes of crisis.

My car, much like Ella's motorcycle, is a sanctuary. It's the physical embodiment of the rhythm and reliability I've come to cherish in my career, an unassuming companion in the tumultuous journey of life. It's carried me through the highs and lows, been my escape when the weight of the world felt too heavy. And today, it seems, is no different.

Stowing away my tools, I catch a glimpse of the time on my watch—the morning has faded. It's almost lunchtime. I'm not training with the team, so the day is mine to do whatever I wish.

I think about Ella. The date cut short.

The thought ignites a surge of guilt within me, despite knowing it wasn't anyone's fault. She'd taken the blame, the pressure, and it churned my insides.

Today, I've got to make it up to her.

With the decision made, I find a quick shower helps rinse away the remnants of the morning's labors, refreshing me for what lies ahead. The cool water washing over me is soothing. It's a moment of respite in a day characterized by thought and action. Soon, it leaves me standing in my kitchen, my mind filled with the task at hand.

Cooking. It's not a skill I often flex, but today, for Ella, it feels like the right time to get my hands dirty.

As a professional soccer player, my relationship with food usually revolves around quick, efficient, and healthy meals. But there's something about preparing a dish for someone else, especially someone you care for, that transforms the act into a labor of love.

Settling on spaghetti aglio e olio, I channel memories of my mother moving around our family kitchen, the image grounding me. I've always loved the simplicity of the dish, the comfort it provides. Garlic, olive oil, red pepper flakes, and parsley—a symphony of flavors harmonizing in an intimate dance.

My hands move almost on their own accord as I follow the steps I've seen performed countless times before. The aroma of sautéed garlic fills my kitchen, an olfactory melody that evokes a sense of nostalgia, a feeling of home.

It's comforting and satisfying. A mirror reflection of my feelings towards Ella.

With the dish complete, I take a moment to admire my work. The spaghetti glistens under the kitchen lights, looking surprisingly appetizing. I take a tentative bite. It's edible. More than edible, it's actually good.

Way to go, Dane.

There's a strange sense of accomplishment in knowing I've created this—that I'm not just Mark, the soccer player, but Mark, the man capable of making a delicious meal for someone special.

Packaging the food, alongside a bottle of red wine, I load up a picnic basket. If I can't whisk Ella away for a joyride on her motorcycle, then I can certainly bring a piece of that adventure to her. The comfort of her office seems like the perfect location for an impromptu lunch date. It will be an oasis amidst the chaos.

My heart pounds with anticipation as I load the picnic basket into the trunk of my car. The hum of the engine, usually so soothing, now echoes the adrenaline-fueled rhythm of my heartbeat. I pull out of the driveway, the road ahead seeming brighter, more alive, and filled with promise.

Nashville disappears and the winding road south to Loveland passes by in a blur, my mind only on one thing.

Ella.

Her surprise when she sees the lunch I've prepared.

The light in her eyes. The smile that I know will break out on her face. Today, I'm not just doing this to lift her spirits, I'm doing it because I want to be the reason behind that smile.

As The Romantics building comes into view, my pulse quickens. It's time for our do-over date. It's nothing grand, but it feels right. Because today, it's not only about the adventure. It's about *her*.

Stepping out of my car, I retrieve the picnic basket, each step towards the building filling me with a sense of purpose. The promise to put a smile on Ella's face resonates within me. As I push through the doors, stepping into the hub of activity, my pulse quickens.

This might just turn out to be the best spontaneous lunch date I've ever planned.

The building is a hive of dynamic chaos, everyone moving with purpose and a dash of desperation. In the eye of the storm, Ella's boutique shines like a beacon.

A woman I presume to be Becca, Ella's assistant, gives me a knowing smile and waves me through. Ella's reputation as an elusive enigma apparently doesn't extend to me. I try not to grin too broadly at the thought. I like being her exception.

Ella's office is a small sanctuary of calm in the rear of the otherwise bustling boutique. An organized chaos, much like the woman herself. Papers are stacked neatly, colored pens are lined like soldiers, and a smattering of delicate trinkets from various places she's been tell a story. Her desk is a monument to multi-tasking, multiple screens humming with activity, notes jotted on sticky notes that flutter at the edges. It's all so ... Ella.

I love it.

And there, framed in the soft light filtering in through the window, is the woman herself.

Her brows are furrowed in concentration. She's biting her lip in that adorable way she does when she's deep in thought. The sight of her instantly eases any lingering nerves, replacing them with a warmth that radiates from my core.

She looks up, her gaze colliding with mine. Her eyes go wide, a look of surprise that quickly morphs into delight. It's the reaction I was hoping for.

"Mark?" she exclaims, quickly standing up. "What are you doing here?"

There's no accusation in her voice, only surprise and curiosity. It encourages me, pushing my nerves aside.

"I come bearing gifts," I say with a grin, hoisting the picnic basket for her to see.

Her eyes flick to the basket and back to my face, confusion clear on her features. "Gifts?"

I nod. "Lunch, to be specific. Spaghetti aglio e olio, handmade by yours truly."

Her eyebrows shoot up, surprise morphing into amazement. "You cooked?"

"At your service," I confirm with a mock bow.

The bubble of laughter that escapes her is music to my ears. It's a sound I could get used to. A sound I want to be the reason for.

Her eyes sparkle with mischief as she asks, "Do I need to be worried about food poisoning?"

I feign shock, placing a hand over my heart. "I'll have you know, I'm a culinary genius."

Her laughter fills the room once again, warming me from the inside out. "Alright, Chef Mark, I'm game."

We settle onto the floor of her office, surrounded by stacks of papers and books, the picnic blanket spread out beneath us. It's unconventional, but somehow it feels so right. It's a space that's uniquely Ella, and it feels like an honor to be invited into it.

We spend the rest of the lunch break in comfortable conversation.

Between bites of spaghetti and sips of wine, we share stories and laughter, each moment binding us closer together. The way her eyes light up when she talks about her work, her passion, it's enthralling. I find myself falling deeper into this strange, beautiful world that is Ella.

I don't realize how much time has passed until her phone buzzes, a reminder of a meeting. She groans, reluctance clear on her face as she glances between me and her phone.

"I hate to cut this short," she says, "but duty calls."

I nod, understanding but a tad disappointed. "Of course. I should probably get going as well."

We pack up, the magic of the moment fading as reality sets back in. She walks me to the door, her expression soft with a touch of regret.

"Thanks for lunch, Mark," she says, her voice barely above a whisper. "It was ... really nice."

I smile, a sense of satisfaction filling me. "I'm glad you enjoyed it."

I really, truly am.

There's a pause, a moment where the world seems to

hold its breath, waiting for what comes next. It's a moment that feels ripe with possibility, a precursor to a question that hangs in the air, unspoken yet profoundly present.

Something about the moment turns me on, and I feel pressure mounting in my pants. Memories of making love to Ella come flooding back. If we stand here much longer, I won't be able to hide my … interest.

Then, Ella shakes her head, a small smile playing on her lips. "I'll see you soon, Mark."

I watch her retreat back into her office, my mind swirling with the potential of those words.

Soon. A promise. A possibility. A single word that propels me forward, into a future where Ella is no longer just a girl who loves adventure, but a woman who might just be willing to embark on one—*another* one—with me.

I'll take it.

As I drive away from The Romantics building, my heart feels lighter and my mind clearer. This is what I want. These moments with Ella, these shared smiles and stories, they're what I've been searching for. They are, in essence, my own version of an adventure.

Back home in Nashville, the quiet of my living room offers a stark contrast to the lively atmosphere of Ella's office. It's a moment of respite, a chance to process the rollercoaster of emotions from the day.

My mind races, thoughts of Ella mixing with my team's upcoming match.

The day may be winding down, but there's a palpable buzz in the air. It's an echo of Ella's vibrant energy, a lingering imprint of our time together. And it's the anticipation of the upcoming game, the thrill of stepping out onto the field, the crowd's roar in my ears.

There's a sense of completeness, and an assurance that I'm right where I'm supposed to be. As I head to bed, I realize that both these aspects of my life, my career and Ella, aren't separate. They're parts of a whole. Parts of me. And as sleep takes over, I'm left with one last thought—tomorrow's match and the prospect of seeing Ella in the crowd, cheering me on.

There's a thrill to that idea, a pulse of excitement that has nothing to do with the game and everything to do with the woman who has started to mean more to me … again.

As sleep claims me, it's not the upcoming match that lulls me into dreams, but the image of Ella's sparkling eyes, her joy-filled laughter, and the promise of many more shared lunches to come.

I can't wait to see what tomorrow brings.

CHAPTER 11

ELLA

The next morning, I arrive at Ever After Bridals, the quaint boutique that's been my labor of love for the past five years. The store's charm lies in its tasteful amalgamation of vintage and modern aesthetics, the rose-gold accents and antique chandeliers juxtaposed with crisp, white walls and clean lines.

It's early, the golden morning light casting long shadows on the quiet Loveland streets.

Unlocking the door, I step into the serene space, the scent of fresh peonies from the corner floral arrangement Rosie made filling my nostrils. I've always believed that the right ambiance can make or break a bridal experience, and today is no different. Even with the chaos of the morning weighing on my shoulders, stepping into my boutique infuses a sense of calm within me. I've spent countless hours transforming this place into a sanctuary, where brides-to-be can turn their dream wedding looks into reality.

A soft chime rings out as I push the door shut

behind me, disrupting the stillness. Becca is already there, going through the day's appointments on her tablet. Her long hair is in a tidy bun today, and she's got her blue-rimmed glasses perched on her nose.

"Morning, boss lady," she greets, not looking up from her screen. Becca has been with me since day one. We've seen Ever After Bridals grow together, weathered the inevitable storms of running a business, and shared more cups of stress-induced coffee than I care to admit.

"Good morning, Becca," I reply, hanging my cardigan on the coat rack and heading towards my office in the back. It's a cozy space, with an oak desk littered with fabric samples, sketch pads, and my trusty sewing machine. It's here that I've sketched countless wedding gowns, each telling a different love story.

Before I can sit down, though, Becca is by my side, her brow furrowed. "Ella, you okay? You seem … off."

I blink at her, surprised. I'd thought I was doing a good job of hiding my stress, but Becca, it seems, knows me too well. I sigh, deciding to be honest with her. "The Romantics," I admit, running a hand through my hair. "There's an issue with the building."

Becca gasps, her hand flying to her chest. She's been by my side throughout the journey, and I know that she understands the significance of this setback. But Becca's a fighter, and within seconds, her surprise morphs into determination. "We'll sort this out, Ella," she declares, her tone brooking no argument.

"You're right. We will."

I spend the morning trying to balance my commitments. Between phone calls with Patrick, going over possible solutions for the building, and attending to the excited brides coming in for their fittings, the hours fly by. It's a chaotic dance, filled with the gentle rustle of silk and satin, the murmur of voices, and the constant pinging of my phone. But this is my element, the place where I thrive.

At lunch, I finally get a moment to breathe. Becca has taken over the store floor, her radiant smile and infectious enthusiasm charming even the most nervous brides. Alone in my office, I chew on my sandwich, my mind drifting to Mark. His laughter, the warmth in his eyes, and his infectious passion for life feel like a balm to my stressed soul.

A smile creeps onto my face, my heart feeling lighter.

I realize then that Mark, in his own quirky way, has become a part of my support system. His presence is like a soothing melody amidst the cacophony of my responsibilities. And as I sit there, lost in thought, I know that I need to make things up to him. I need to show him that he's valued, not just as a blast from the past, but as an integral part of my present.

With renewed vigor, I throw myself back into work, Becca and I moving in perfect tandem to manage the store. The challenges with the building feel less daunting, the weight on my shoulders feeling a tad lighter. There's a sense of hope bubbling within me. A certainty that we will overcome this hurdle, and come out stronger on the other side.

As the day winds down, the afternoon sun bathing my boutique in soft hues of gold and orange, I wrap up.

My heart is full, the rollercoaster of emotions having settled into a steady rhythm. There's an exciting challenge awaiting us, and I know we're ready to face it head-on.

Locking up the boutique, I think about Mark, and the promise of a motorcycle ride. He said he'd be free after his match, and that we could get together.

The thought brings a flutter to my heart, a sense of anticipation that I haven't felt in a while. After all, every time we see each other, it's a chance at a fresh start, and I'm more than ready for mine.

Bring it, universe.

Later, the warmth of the summer night wraps around me as I step out of my townhouse, anticipation thrumming in my veins. Mark is on his way.

There's a sense of familiarity in this moment. The same excitement that used to stir in me back when Mark and I were young and reckless, racing down the Long Island roads without a care in the world.

I'm dressed for the occasion. A breezy tank top and black jeans hug my figure, my hair swept up in a loose bun. In my hands, my motorcycle helmet feels like an old friend, its steady weight promising an evening filled with a familiar thrill.

The distant rumble of an engine slices through the quiet night, and I can't help the small flutter in my stomach. Mark is here. Our past few encounters since bumping into each other at the Nashville bar have been a rollercoaster of emotions—the shock of the reunion, the nostalgia of old memories, and the surprising ease

with which we fell back into our comfortable camaraderie.

Still, tonight feels different, a throwback to our old
summer nights on Long Island.

I'm not even sure why. It just does.

Mark pulls up in his car, the headlights cutting a
swath through the darkness. He steps out, all casual
charm and confidence, a sight that would have sent my
younger self swooning. Today, it only adds to the familiarity of the moment, yet it feels different.

This isn't the Mark from college. This Mark is a
grown man, with a maturity that adds a new dimension
to him.

But okay, who am I kidding? The sight sends my
current self swooning as well. Mark Dane is smoking hot.

He looks at me, his eyes sparkling in the dim light, a
small smile playing on his lips. "Ready for a ride down
memory lane?" he asks, his voice a warm ripple in the
summer night.

I nod, a similar smile tugging at my lips. It's like
stepping back in time, and yet, it's not. We're not the
same people we were back then. We're adults, navigating our way through a rekindled connection, while
remaining rooted in the present.

I'm glad things didn't work out with my MindMate
date, Wes. I would have hated to miss this.

I walk to my motorcycle, the cool metal a contrast to
the warm summer air. I can feel Mark's eyes on me, an
echo of the shared glances from our past. But tonight, it
isn't about looking back. It's about moving forward,

rediscovering each other amidst the familiar thrill of a shared ride.

With a rev of the engine, the night comes alive, the thrill of the ride promising an exciting end to the evening. I glance back at Mark, and his nod signals his readiness. A moment later, we're cruising down the quiet streets of Loveland.

I could get used to this.

The past may have been beautiful, but the promise of the present holds a new allure. After all, this isn't just about recreating old memories. It's about creating new ones, a ride at a time. And I can't wait to see where this journey takes us.

This ride isn't just about revisiting the past. It's a metaphor for us, for Mark and me. How we're navigating a new path together, building on our past, but racing towards a future that is thrilling in its own right.

As the lights of small-town Loveland turn into a hazy glow in the rearview mirror, I anticipate the rest of the evening, ready to dive headfirst into this exciting new chapter of our story.

The summer night feels full of promise.

Just like the open road in front of me, our story is unfolding, one moment, one mile at a time. I'm excited about the journey that lies ahead. As the wind whips through my hair and I breathe in Mark's familiar, woodsy scent, I smile.

Here's to new beginnings. Here's to us.

CHAPTER 12

ELLA

There's nothing quite like waking up on a Sunday in a town where you know everyone but everyone also knows you. A place where the line between personal life and public knowledge is more blurred than the edge of a watercolor painting.

Welcome to Loveland.

The smell of brewing coffee greets me before I open my eyes. I stretch, my body aching pleasantly from last night's ride. I'm content, my mind still wrapped in a dreamy haze, replaying the echo of Mark's laughter and the warm pressure of my arm around his waist.

I rise from my bed, the cool hardwood floor beneath my bare feet a welcome contrast to the warm summer morning. My townhouse is modest, brimming with the comfort of familiarity, every piece of furniture holding a story of my past, every wall adorned with a mosaic of my dreams and memories.

After a quick shower, I pull on my favorite denim shorts and a loose, white blouse, my hair still damp as I make my way downstairs to my quaint kitchen. The coffee machine, as if sensing my need, pours out the last bit of black gold into the pot. A whiff of the rich aroma and I already feel more awake, more ready to face another day in my life.

As I sip on my coffee, my phone buzzes. It's a text from Becca, reminding me about a shipment of wedding dresses we're expecting at the boutique today. Becca has become not just an indispensable part of my work life, but a dear friend as well.

Checking the time, I realize I've got some hours before I need to head to the boutique. The morning sun paints golden streaks across the sky, the day unfolding with a lazy elegance. I decide to spend some time in my tiny yet lush garden, a sanctuary of tranquility amidst the buzz of small-town life.

As I step out, the soft chirping of birds greets me, the light breeze causing the wind chimes to sing a harmonious melody.

With a mug of coffee in one hand and a book in the other, I settle onto my favorite garden chair, the soft cushions enveloping me comfortably. The book is a romance novel, the promise of a happy ending fueling my curiosity. As I get lost in the pages, I can't help but draw parallels between the unfolding story and my own blossoming romance with Mark.

The thought brings a smile to my face, a flutter to my heart.

The morning passes in peaceful solitude, the world outside my garden taking its own course. At the back of my mind, I am aware of the day's responsibilities. My serene morning is about to get busy with the chaos of wedding dress fittings and consultations. Yet for now, I enjoy the tranquility of the moment, the warm sun, the soft rustle of leaves, the distant laughter of children playing on the sidewalk.

A buzz from my phone pulls me from my reverie. It's another text from Becca, confirming that the shipment has left Nashville and will reach us within an hour. She's also included a series of wedding dress photos for my perusal. Becca's eye for detail and excellent taste in fashion have saved the day more times than I can count.

With a sigh, I close my book and finish the last dregs of my now cold coffee. The comfort of my garden chair is reluctantly abandoned as I head back inside to prepare for the day at Ever After Bridals. In this business, working weekends is a given.

As I swap my casual attire for a more professional outfit, a small part of me is already looking forward to tonight's dinner with Mark. But before I can get lost in daydreams of a romantic evening, I need to tackle the exciting chaos that waits for me at the boutique.

Closing the door behind me, I mount my motorcycle, the familiar hum beneath me a thrill that never gets old. As I ride toward the boutique, the wind playing with my hair, I feel a buzz of anticipation for the day. Little did I know that the day would hold more surprises than just a new shipment of wedding dresses. The ride, however, is a story for another time. For now, I'm just a woman, ready to conquer her day, one bridal gown at a time.

CHAPTER 13

MARK

*I*t's evening, and I'm waiting for her in Downtown Loveland.

The chatter of the crowd and the upbeat country music fade into a soft hum as I watch Ella make her way towards me.

Be still, my heart.

Huh. I sound like some kind of hopeless romantic. Maybe I am.

The moonlight filtering through the canopies above us casts an ethereal glow, making her look other-worldly. Her blonde hair shines as if woven with threads of gold. Her emerald eyes sparkle with a mischief that's become my favorite thing to decipher. She's walking with purpose, her hands clenched tightly at her sides.

She's nervous. *Good.*

"Mark Dane, always a sight for sore eyes," she begins, her voice a luscious mix of sarcasm and warmth that sends a thrill through me. It's the same voice I remember from our summer together, only now, it's more matured, more confident.

I'm still riding high on the thrill of memories mixed with current-day admiration … and attraction. My jeans tighten against my growing bulge. I can't help it.

"Only for sore eyes, Ella?" I tease, relishing the way her name rolls off my tongue.

Her eyes narrow, but there's a playfulness in her gaze. "Especially for sore eyes," she corrects herself, and a laugh escapes her lips. The sound resonates through the night, outshining the music and the chatter.

For a moment, I consider leaning down to kiss her. But I don't. The last thing I'd want to do is rush things and make her uncomfortable.

Ella Lovelace is worth waiting for.

"How was your day?" she asks, her tone casual as if we haven't just spent the past week caught in a whirlwind of emotions. I shrug nonchalantly, but my heart is thumping.

"Same old. Most days, it's a half-day training session, then a press meet or charity function," I answer. "With a few days off in the mix."

It's a half-truth, though. The soccer field and the additional duties are the least of my worries. What's been keeping me up at night is the woman standing in front of me.

"That sounds … exciting," she replies, but the corners of her lips twitch, indicating her blatant sarcasm.

Ella's always had a way of making the ordinary seem extraordinary, and the extraordinary, well, ordinary.

"Only if you're there," I quip, earning myself a

surprised chuckle. "I've been hoping you'd show up at a game." But Ella being Ella, she recovers quickly.

"Are you flirting with me, Dane?" she asks, trying to sound stern, but the twinkle in her eyes betrays her.

"Only if it's working," I shoot back, leaning in just a little closer. The moonlight illuminates her face, highlighting her rosy cheeks. Ella takes a step back, feigning shock, and I laugh, enjoying this dance between us.

"I'm immune to your charms, remember?" she retorts, but her voice is softer now, almost wistful.

"That's what you keep telling yourself," I tease. I can see her cheeks reddening, and it brings me an unexplainable joy.

Our banter continues, the laughter and playful nudges filling the space between us with an intoxicating warmth. It feels as if we're the only two people in this crowded square. But then, the moment is broken when Ella's gaze shifts over my shoulder, her eyebrows furrowing slightly.

I turn around to see what's caught her attention and spot a man standing a few feet away. His gaze is fixed on Ella with a strange intensity, his hands shoved into his pockets. A sense of unease creeps up my spine, the man's presence bringing an unwanted tension to our comfortable camaraderie. But before I can say anything, he turns around and disappears into the crowd.

When I look back at Ella, her eyes are wide and her face is pale. She's visibly shaken. "Ella, do you know that guy?" I ask, my voice laced with concern. She shakes her head, brushing off my question with a forced laugh.

"No, it's nothing. Just ... he reminded me of someone," she says. But her voice is shaky, and she's avoiding my gaze. Something is not right.

Come to think of it, he kind of looked like the guy she was with when we bumped into each other at the Nashville bar last week. She'd said she was on a date, set up via a dating app. I wonder if she's interested in that guy?

Do I have competition?

Before I can probe further, she quickly changes the subject. "I'm thirsty. Let's get something to drink," she suggests, her voice back to its cheery self. But I can tell she's forcing it.

I nod, deciding to let it go for now. "Sure, Ella. Whatever you say."

As we head towards The Spotted Lilly, I fear that something is about to change. The comfortable ease we'd fallen into feels threatened, and the uncertainty of it all leaves me on edge.

Even so, I keep my worries to myself, vowing to keep Ella's smile intact. Because right now, that's all that matters. I'll deal with the rest later. As for the next step —well, I guess we'll find out soon enough.

There's an unspoken promise hanging in the air between us, a promise of a future we're both willing to fight for. And as we delve deeper into the night, wrapped in our bubble, I feel hopeful. Because as long as Ella is by my side, everything else can wait.

CHAPTER 14

ELLA

The Tennessee sun is a powerful thing. Not just for the way it turns the grass a dazzling shade of emerald or the way it paints strokes of gold across the Loveland skyline, but for how it amplifies everything—every emotion, every sensation, and every single flutter in my heart when I see Mark.

It's the next day, and I'm stepping out from Ever After Bridals, a whirlwind of lace and tulle left behind me, my boutique alive with the bustle of upcoming weddings. The summer air hums with the fragrance of blooming honeysuckle, mixing with the enticing scent of Cece's bakery nearby.

Closing my eyes, I take a moment to soak in the serenity. Serenity is a relative term, of course, especially when your heart beats like a runaway drum, and your mind is a constant stream of Mark-Dane-thoughts.

When I open my eyes, there he is, pulling into the parking lot in his sporty coupe. He steps out, as sleek and alluring as his car, his deep brown hair tousled in a perfectly 'I just woke up looking like a model' manner. His shirt clings to his torso in a way that should be declared illegal, highlighting his well-honed physique.

"Damn," I mutter under my breath, making the sign of the cross. "Lead us not into temptation."

I'm still fasting, after all. Remember?

With a bouquet of peonies in his hand, he strolls towards me, a teasing smile playing on his lips. "But isn't temptation much more fun, Ella?" he asks, handing me the flowers. His voice, rough with a hint of humor, sends a jolt through me.

"Why, Mark Dane, are you eavesdropping on a girl's private conversation with herself?" I laugh, accepting the flowers, my heart doing cartwheels in my chest.

We head over to a bench under a sprawling oak tree. He sits close enough that our knees brush against each other. It's a minuscule touch, yet it sends tidal waves through me. I find myself leaning into him, our bodies drawn to each other like opposite poles of magnets.

"Are you okay?" Mark asks, his voice laced with concern. "You seem ... lost."

Do I confess how I'm lost in the whirlpool of our past and present, the sharp edges of our history gradually being smoothed out by these little moments we're sharing now?

"Just pondering," I answer, giving him a small smile.

He nods, a tiny furrow between his brows, and it's clear he's not entirely convinced. But he leaves it at that. It's a strange dance we're in—weaving around the reality of our past, the palpable connection in our present, the looming question of our future. All set against the warm, golden backdrop of a Loveland summer day.

"So," I begin, trying to bring back the lightness in our conversation. "Did you get lost on your way to a date and end up in a flower shop?"

He laughs, the sound radiating warmth. "Actually, these flowers are for you. Just a little something to brighten your day."

"Mark Dane, are you trying to woo me?"

He shrugs, a playful glint in his eyes. "Is it working?"

And even though I chuckle, brushing it off with a playful nudge, I can't ignore the flutter in my heart.

His boyish charm is a dangerous thing. More dangerous than the Tennessee sun. Because while the sun can turn the grass emerald and the skies gold, Mark Dane has the power to color my world in hues I thought I'd forgotten.

A thrill runs through me as I consider the evening ahead, the local festival, the Loveland Country Carnival, that has the whole of our little town buzzing with excitement. There will be lights, music, and shared secrets under the cover of darkness.

There will be Mark and me, together.

Even as I pretend to chide him for his flirtatious ways, I can't help but wonder, could this be our second chance? Could this bright, beautiful day be the official dawn of a new beginning for us?

I guess only time will tell.

CHAPTER 15

MARK

It's evening again, and I'm under the spell of the Loveland Country Carnival.

The small town vibe reminds me of growing up on Long Island. Oyster Bay, New York, where I'm from and where my dad still lives, has a similar feel to it, believe it or not. The surroundings are quaint and the neighbors are friendly in both places.

Tonight, Ella's got me wrapped around her little finger tighter than a guitar string, and honestly, I wouldn't have it any other way. She's as intoxicating as the Tennessee moonshine, and the more I'm around her, the more I want.

Her laughter rings out over the hum of the crowd, the lights from the festival booths playing with the gold strands of her hair. The night is alive with the smells of fried food, the neon glow of rides, and the exhilarating thrill of being here, in this moment with Ella.

The taste of cotton candy lingers on my lips, a sweet reminder of a stolen kiss under the cover of the vibrant festival lights. It was a small kiss. A peck, really. But it has me red hot with desire. Her mouth felt like home.

She's by my side, her hand nestled securely in mine, fitting perfectly like the missing piece of a puzzle. My heart thumps erratically in my chest, a wild rhythm matching the vibrant country music blaring from the stage. With every passing minute, I'm falling deeper, and the funny thing is, I'm not even trying to resist.

"Come on," she says, tugging my hand, her eyes sparkling brighter than the Ferris wheel spinning lazily in the distance. "I want to show you something."

We weave through the crowd, her laughter leaving a trail of melody in the air. She pulls me towards a shooting booth, her eyes glinting with an untamed joy that's nothing short of infectious.

"Best out of three?" she challenges, a playful smirk on her face.

A chuckle escapes me. "You're on, blondie."

She sticks her tongue out at me, a childlike gesture that adds another layer to my ever-growing fascination with this woman. Not to mention, I remember how that tongue feels, and what it can do. I adjust my jeans, the fabric tightening.

We take our turns, the game ending with Ella hitting two out of three and me, well, I'll admit it's not my finest hour.

Her peals of laughter fill the air, the sound sweeter than any prize I could have won. "Looks like you owe me a prize, Mr. Dane."

"A deal's a deal," I reply, my heart light. "What'll it be?"

"Hmm," she ponders, her finger tapping against her lips in a manner that sends my mind spiraling. She points towards a giant stuffed bunny at the corner of the prize booth. "That one!"

"And here I thought you'd ask for the moon," I say, reaching for the plush toy.

"Who says I won't ask for that next?" she teases, her fingers brushing against mine as she takes the bunny. The touch sends electric jolts through me, a startling reminder of the growing tension between us.

The rest of the night is a blur of laughter, shared cotton candy kisses, and unspoken confessions. It's a night of stolen moments, whispered promises, and the hauntingly beautiful possibility of what could be.

We cap it off with a slow dance under the starlit sky, Ella wrapped in my arms, her body swaying with mine in perfect rhythm.

I think I've died and gone to heaven.

"I had a great time, Mark," she whispers, her head resting against my chest, her voice sending ripples through my heart. "Thank you."

"No, thank you, Ella," I reply, my voice barely above a whisper. "For reminding me what it feels like ... to live."

As the night draws to an end, and we part ways with a promise to see each other tomorrow, I reflect on what just happened. On the undeniable bond between us that seems to grow stronger with each passing moment.

Yes, there are questions to be answered and uncertainties to be addressed. But tonight, under the soft glow of the Loveland Country Carnival, with the taste of Ella's cotton candy kisses still on my lips, everything seems possible.

A new chapter awaits, and with it, the hope of unraveling the beautiful mystery that is Ella. A mystery I'm more than ready to dive into, headfirst. Because if tonight is anything to go by, I'm in for a hell of a ride, one that promises to be sweeter than any cotton candy and brighter than any festival light.

Tonight, I've caught a glimpse of what could be, of a future with Ella that seems within reach. As I walk away from the festival grounds, a part of me holds onto the thrill of what tomorrow might bring. Because if there's one thing I've learned tonight, it's that with Ella, even the ordinary can turn into an adventure. And I'm ready for the ride of a lifetime.

With the echoes of the festival slowly fading into the night, I turn my car towards home, my heart filled with anticipation. A silent promise for tomorrow hangs in the air.

Even though we're heading into uncharted territory, for the first time in a long time, I feel grounded, as if I'm exactly where I'm meant to be.

With Ella.

CHAPTER 16

ELLA

The morning sun, warm and encouraging, streams through the blinds, painting stripes of light and shadow on the floor of my townhouse. But I'm still half asleep, caught up in a dream … a sexy one.

I roll away from the window, pulling the covers over my head. I'm too immersed—and aroused—to let this end. Not yet.

In my dream world, Mark and I are back on Long Island, just like that glorious summer during college. We're at Jones Beach State Park, walking along the boardwalk. It's evening in my dream. No one else is around. That part isn't exactly true to life as it's usually busy. For now, though, my mind wants it to be just the two of us.

I'm loving it.

As we stroll hand in hand, me in a string bikini and him in body-hugging board shorts, Dream Mark glances around, making sure no one is watching. Once he confirms that the coast is clear, he grabs my hand

and pulls me down some stairs that lead to a private alcove under the boardwalk. Water laps gently at our ankles as he leans me back against the weathered wood then props one hand above my head.

"What's this about?" I ask in the dream, only I don't really care what he replies.

He buries his head into my neck, nibbling seductively as he speaks. "It's about you. And me."

"Umm," I groan, and I think I actually make the sound in real life.

Dream Mark doesn't give me time to protest. He moves his mouth down my body, planting kisses as he goes. I lean my head back and close my eyes, every inch of me ready for him. I want him. Desperately.

"Is this okay?" he asks.

I nod emphatically. "Umm hmm," I moan. "More."

I feel his cheeks tighten into a smile as he moves the fabric of my bikini top with his tongue, then he uses that magnificent tongue to encircle one erect nipple. Meanwhile, he takes both hands and grabs my hips, pulling me close against him. His grip is tight, but not too tight.

Waves of pleasure course through my body. Suddenly, something comes over me and I'm like a woman possessed. I reach out and tear at his shorts, my hand possessing more strength than I knew I had.

"Take them off," I breathe.

He laughs, that mischievous laugh I've come to love so much. "You don't have to tell me twice," he says as he scoots out of his shorts, exposing his rock hard appendage that appears to be as eager for me as I am for it.

Slowly, he unties the bikini string that sits on my hip, then he slides one warm palm between my legs, shrugging the bikini bottom off. It falls to the sand below us. I give it a little kick for good measure.

Now, skin to skin, I let my hands and my body do what they want. I act on pure animal instinct, and Mark does the same.

We squeeze and pull on each other hungrily, the sounds of the gentle waves acting as a romantic backdrop for the most sensual experience of my life.

Although, I take that back. Every time with Mark feels like the most sensual experience of my life. None of the men I've been with since could hold a candle to what it feels like when I'm with him. Maybe that's why I've slept with so many. Maybe I'm chasing that high, wishing to relive what felt right and true … and mind-blowingly amazing.

As Dream Mark lifts me and I wrap my legs around his waist, the pressure builds between my legs in real life. I'm going to come, right here in my bed … alone. And I want it. I want to. This fast has been incredibly difficult. Seeing Mark and not taking him to bed has been torture.

Ugh.

I close my eyes tighter and let it happen.

Dream Mark slides inside of me, and I remember what a perfect fit we are together. His manhood is the perfect size and shape to fill me up while still being agile enough to move into positions that hit all the right spots. He kisses me deeply and stimulates my nipples while rhythmically pumping and grinding into the deepest parts of me.

It takes less than a minute. I come so hard that my entire body coils and writhes with pleasure.

Oh, Mark. My Mark.

Once I've relaxed and opened my eyes fully, I push off the soft sheets, savoring the quiet hum of Loveland waking up around me. My body still tingles, and not just from the orgasm. Last night has me walking on air.

I'm still thinking about the sweet thrum of country music, the pulsing lights, and the intoxicating scent of cotton candy mixed with the fresh summer air. Most of all, I'm thinking about Mark's laughter, a sound I thought I had forgotten, now replaying on an endless loop in my mind.

I swing my legs over the edge of the bed, taking a moment to stretch and enjoy the peaceful morning before the rest of my day gets going. I hear the gentle rustling of scales and turn to see Gonzo, lazily coiling and uncoiling in his enclosure.

"Morning, Gonzo," I say, grinning at his inquisitive flickering tongue. I feed him his favorite breakfast treat, a thawed mouse, and he slithers over with an eagerness that makes me laugh. I suppose everyone, even a snake, appreciates a good breakfast.

After showering, I pad barefoot down the stairs and into the kitchen, pulling on my favorite faded jeans and a tank top. I set the coffee maker to brew, and the rich aroma soon fills the room. Sipping the strong black liquid, I lean against the countertop, my mind wandering back to Mark.

Mark Dane.

The man who set my heart on fire one summer in college and then left with barely a word, leaving only heartache behind. The man who unexpectedly walked back into my life, the years in between seeming to evaporate in an instant. The man who, last night, looked at me in a way that made me believe in second chances.

Our moment on the Ferris wheel, suspended high above the Loveland Country Carnival, was unexpected. The world shrunk to the tiny enclosed space around us, his hand warm on mine, the shared laughter and reminiscing giving way to something more profound. And then, a passionate kiss. A tender collision of past and present, regret and hope.

And now? I'm not quite sure.

I take a final gulp of my coffee, shaking my head to clear away the daydreams.

It's a beautiful Monday morning and I've got things to do. I'm heading out to the local farmers market, a weekly tradition I never miss. I love the vibrant array of produce, the scent of fresh flowers, the cheerful chatter of vendors and shoppers. It's a grounding ritual that brings me back to reality and I need it today, especially after the whirlwind of last night.

I lock up my townhouse, throwing a wave to Mrs. Jenkins next door who's always up early tending to her flower garden. Her Boston Terrier, Pippa, gives me a cheerful bark, wagging her little tail. I walk down the street, the air around me brimming with summer delights.

Mark's ghost trails behind me, a warm presence I cannot shake.

The market is abuzz with activity by the time I arrive. I wander through the bustling rows, greeting familiar faces. The local honey from the Jameson Farm, Cece Baker's cherry pies from Queen of Tarts, and the fresh sourdough from the Andersons. There's comfort in the familiar, and I bask in it.

"Hey, Ella," Charlie, the friendly greengrocer, calls out, waving me over to his stall. I select the juiciest peaches and crisp lettuce, dropping them into my reusable bag.

"So, how was the carnival last night?" Charlie asks with a teasing grin.

Word travels fast in a small town like Loveland. At least no one knows about my sexy dream.

I feel my cheeks warm. "The carnival was good," I manage to say. "Really good."

Charlie chuckles, a twinkle in his eyes. "Sounds like more than just good."

I roll my eyes playfully, nudging him with my elbow.

He's right, of course. It was much more than good. But the fact that even Charlie senses a change in me is a little unnerving.

I finish my shopping, chatting and laughing with the market regulars, but my thoughts are elsewhere, floating somewhere between the twinkling lights of the carnival and a certain pair of deep blue eyes ... and just maybe a boardwalk at Jones Beach State Park on Long Island.

Suddenly, the sound of my phone chiming in my bag jolts me back to the present moment. I fish it out, my heart skipping a beat as I see the name on the screen.

Mark.

"See you at the game tonight?" His text reads.

A wide grin spreads across my face, igniting a glow that I suspect will last the entire day. I punch in a quick reply, "Wouldn't miss it for the world."

He's been wanting me to attend a game, and I can't wait to do so. I want to see him in his element.

As I leave the market, the day suddenly seems brighter, the colors more vibrant, and the summer air even sweeter. Tonight, I'm going to watch Mark Dane play professional soccer. And somehow, I have a feeling it's going to be more than just good.

Much, much more.

Later, I stand in front of my mirror, deliberating over my outfit for the evening. The soccer match is due to begin in a few hours. I opt for a pair of cut-off jean shorts and a blue and white striped off-the-shoulder top. It's a comfortable, yet fashionable, ensemble. Just right for a warm summer night.

As I fuss with my hair, my phone vibrates on the bed. It's a text from Rosie. Her message reads, "So, it's a night with the hunky Mark Dane, huh?" Her teasing tone seeps through the screen, drawing a chuckle from me.

"Nothing like that, Rosie," I quickly type back, my heart fluttering at the suggestion.

The idea of a 'we' between Mark and me? It feels as tantalizing as it does frightening.

Shaking my head, I check on Gonzo and leave my townhouse, the thrill of the evening ahead of me already prickling at my senses.

When I arrive, the atmosphere at the Geodis Park is electric. An excited hum of chatter and laughter fills the air, the echoes of anticipation and camaraderie palpable.

I make my way to my seat, which Mark suggested would offer the best view of the field. As I catch sight of Mark in his soccer gear, my heart gallops in my chest. Even from a distance, he exudes an air of confidence that is almost tangible. Not to mention, he is objectively gorgeous.

He is certainly not the shy boy I once knew. Although, that boy is still in there, somewhere.

The match commences and the stadium springs to life. There's a collective intake of breath as the players move swiftly, and the rhythmic thud of the ball against the turf reverberates in my ears. Mark is nothing short of impressive, his athleticism clearly on display. Every swift movement, every calculated kick, is a testament to his talent and passion for the sport. I find myself cheering enthusiastically, the excitement in the air infectious.

When there's a pause and Mark steps off the pitch, my phone vibrates in my pocket, pulling me away from the game momentarily. A text from Mark glows on the screen. "Look to your left."

Surprised, I follow his instruction. A few rows away

stands a man I recognize as Mark's trainer, Peter. He gives me a friendly wave and a warm smile. "Mark wanted someone to keep you company!" he shouts over the noise of the crowd. I laugh, touched by Mark's thoughtfulness, and wave back.

The game resumes its fierce pace and before I know it, the final whistle blows. The Nashville SC team emerges victorious and the stadium resonates with applause and cheers. I join in, my heart bursting with pride for Mark and his teammates.

As the crowd starts to thin, Peter approaches me. "Mark has some press commitments to attend to," he explains, pointing towards a side door. "He asked if you'd like to wait for him in the players' lounge."

The offer is tempting, to say the least. It's a chance to glimpse a part of Mark's world I've never seen before. A part of me hesitates, but the thrill of this new adventure drowns out any lingering doubts.

With a determined smile, I nod at Peter. "Lead the way."

The evening has already offered a taste of exhilarating experiences and as I follow Peter towards the players' lounge, I can't quell the anticipation thrumming within me. Tonight promises a closer look into Mark's life off the field and the prospect is as nerve-wracking as it is exciting.

As the door to the lounge swings open, I steel myself for what the night has yet to reveal.

I feel so … alive.

CHAPTER 17

MARK

The final whistle has blown, our victory solidifying in the echoing sound that bounces off the grandstand walls of Geodis Park. My body is buzzing, the last remnants of adrenaline still lighting up my nerves even as the game becomes a memory. But my mind? My mind is elsewhere, on the woman whose eyes haven't left me for the entirety of the match.

Unfortunately, I have press commitments. The necessary evil of every match.

After the first few years, you learn to deal with it, an art form in dodging sensitive questions and delivering just enough charm to keep them coming back for more. Tonight though, the words are a little more hollow than usual. The sparkle I'm normally able to bring to the camera feels a bit dimmer. Because Ella is waiting. And every moment I'm not with her feels like an opportunity missed.

I finally excuse myself from the press, my eyes

immediately scanning the crowd for her. There she is, next to Peter Daniels, my trainer, a charismatic man in his mid-50s who's never met a stranger he didn't like. I walk towards them, my heart pounding in a way that has nothing to do with the game I've just played.

"Great game, Mark. You were on fire tonight!" Ella's smile reaches her eyes, lighting them up in a way that has me thinking ridiculous things, like how I'd love to be the reason for her smiles every day.

She's a vision, the evening light catching the soft waves of her blonde hair.

The conversation flows with an ease that feels natural, not just between Ella and me, but with Peter too. It's easy to forget the difference in our ages, as his youthful spirit easily bridges the gap. Laughter, jokes, shared stories of memorable games, Peter has them all in his arsenal. But just as I'm getting lost in the moment, Peter changes the game.

"Remember New York, Mark?" His voice is still light, his smile still in place, but the underlying seriousness in his eyes is hard to miss.

My laugh falters, the ghosts of the past emerging from the shadows. The laughter around me dims, my focus narrowing down to the memories that the simple question has stirred up. But Peter's reminder isn't meant to be harsh, I know this. He's looking out for me, trying to warn me of the storm that might be on the horizon if I don't address my past.

For a moment, the specter of my past in Long Island looms large, casting a shadow on the enjoyable evening. But then, I look at Ella. Her eyes are full of warmth and something more, something that tells me that maybe it's time to confront those demons.

Peter's warning isn't meant to scare me away from Ella. Quite the opposite. It's a push to face my past so that I can have a future. A future that I'm beginning to hope includes Ella.

He's right.

Peter and I met back when I was in college as a young player at Boston College. In fact, he followed me here to Nashville. He knows my story. He was there to see it unfold.

"How could I forget?" I reply.

He nods, giving me a knowing wink and a smile.

As the evening winds down, Peter's words linger in the air. His advice, though unsolicited, has given me something to think about. It has made me realize that if I want to see where this connection with Ella goes, I need to confront my past first. I can't let my history in New York remain a ghost that haunts me. It's time to exorcise those demons, and maybe, just maybe, Ella is the one person who can help me do that.

It's an intimidating thought, but the look in Ella's eyes gives me hope. Hope that, with her by my side, I can face anything. So as we say our goodbyes for the evening, I can't help but feel excited for what comes next. Peter's words have marked the beginning of a new chapter in my life, and I'm eager to see what it holds.

As I head home, my mind is filled with thoughts of Ella.

I think about her laugh, her passion, and the way her eyes light up when she talks about her bridal designs. I think about how she looked at me tonight, not as a soccer player, but as Mark, the man behind the jersey. And most importantly, I think about my past and the journey I need to undertake to confront it.

My life has always revolved around soccer, but tonight, I realize it's about to include so much more. And that, more than anything else, makes me feel like I've truly won tonight. Not just the game, but something far more precious. A chance at a future that holds more than just soccer. A chance at a future with Ella. It's an exhilarating thought, one that fills me with anticipation and an eagerness to see what tomorrow holds. Because now, it's not just about soccer.

As the night closes in, I find myself looking forward to tomorrow. Because tomorrow, I'll see Ella again. And who knows? Maybe tomorrow, we'll start our journey together. A journey to confront the past, celebrate the present, and build a future.

I can't wait to see where it takes us.

Later, after finally peeling myself out of the car and managing the front door, I'm greeted by the comforting silence of my own home. It's a tall, narrow house in the Hillsboro neighborhood, characteristic of the Nashville residential architectural style and referred to as a tall skinny. Within its sleek, modern walls, it's all Mark Dane.

I love my home. Every carefully selected piece of furniture, every fixture, every bit of decor. It's mine, and it's more than just a house—it's a sanctuary.

The weight of the evening starts to press against my shoulders as I close the door behind me, the outside world shut out with a satisfying click of the lock. The glow from the streetlights filters in through the tall windows, casting long, shadowy shapes on the floor. There's a comfort in this quiet solitude, in the familiar hum of the fridge, in the soft, well-worn rug beneath my bare feet.

I wander through the open living space, past the modern couch and glass coffee table, my mind adrift with thoughts of the game, the win, and Ella. Always Ella. There's a certain thrill to it all, the joy of victory, the satisfaction of a game well played, but it's the thought of seeing her again that has my heart thumping in my chest.

As I start up the stairs to the bedroom, my phone buzzes in my pocket. I pull it out to see a text from Rosie. It's a photo of Ella at the game tonight, laughing with Peter, a Nashville SC scarf wrapped around her neck. Rosie has captioned it with, "Your biggest fan."

Huh. I didn't know Rosie had my number, but I'm glad she does.

I smile, warmth spreading through me. There's a light in Ella's eyes, a joy that seems to shine right through the screen. I quickly type back, "I'm a lucky man," before switching off my phone. I don't need the rest of the world right now. Right now, it's enough to be home, to bask in the memory of Ella's laughter and her sparkling eyes.

As I flop onto the bed, my body groaning with the toll of the day's exertions, I replay the game in my head. The cheers of the crowd, the adrenaline rush of each goal, the thrill of victory. But as satisfying as the win is, it pales in comparison to the prospect of seeing Ella tomorrow. There's a tension to it, a sense of anticipation that keeps me awake long after my body has begged for rest.

Tomorrow, I'll face Long Island. I'll face my past. But knowing that Ella will be there, waiting for me, makes it all seem a little less daunting. It's a battle I'm ready to fight, a hurdle I'm willing to jump. Because at the end of it all is Ella, with her infectious laughter, her warm eyes, and that indescribable something that draws me in.

This has been a long time coming. It's something that needs to happen.

I close my eyes, the tension slowly draining away. The house settles around me, the silence a comforting blanket. Tomorrow is another day, filled with promises and challenges. But for now, in the soft, quiet dark of my Nashville home, it's enough to be Mark Dane. Not the Nashville SC star, but just Mark, the man who's found something—*someone*—worth fighting for.

With that thought, I let the peaceful quiet of the night carry me away.

CHAPTER 18

ELLA

The morning rays filter through the blinds of my bedroom, landing directly on my face. As I crack one eye open, I find my phone buzzing on the nightstand. Who could be calling this early? I groan, taking a peek at the screen.

It's Mark.

"Good morning, sunshine," he greets, sounding irritatingly chipper for this ungodly hour.

"Mark, it's 7 a.m. What are you doing?" I grumble into the phone, rolling onto my side, away from the offending light.

"I just finished my morning workout, and I thought of a great idea," he says, the excitement in his voice almost palpable.

I rub my eyes, trying to shake off the remnants of sleep. "Okay, I'm listening."

"I was thinking we could take a trip to Long Island. You know, like old times."

The words jolt me fully awake. A trip to Long

Island? "Mark, that's ... wow, I mean, it's been years," I stammer, my heart pounding in my chest.

Long Island isn't just any place. It's where we first met, where we spent our summer during college, where we fell in love, and ultimately, where we fell apart.

"Yeah, it has. But I think it's time, don't you? Time to face the past, reminisce a bit?" he suggests, his tone calm and steady, the complete opposite of the whirlwind of emotions churning inside me. "I have some time off work before the season officially begins. No matches for the week. Can you get away?"

"I ... yes, I think that could be good," I reply, my voice barely more than a whisper. "I might have to work on my laptop while we're away. I don't know. I'll need to talk to Becca. We don't have anything major on the books. She can probably hold down the fort."

"Great! I'll arrange everything. We can fly out next weekend," Mark says. I can practically hear the smile in his voice.

A small smile tugs at my lips as I hang up. The day just started, but my mind is already filled with a whirl-wind of emotions. This trip to Long Island could be a turning point for us, a chance to rekindle the flame that we let die all those years ago. Or it could just be another heartbreak waiting to happen.

Only time will tell.

I hop out of bed and make my way to the shower, the hot water washing away my worries. A chance to revisit our past isn't something I should be scared of. It's an opportunity, a second chance. And as I let the water cascade over me, I let myself imagine what could be.

Ahh.

Stepping out of the shower, I wrap myself in a fluffy towel and head to the kitchen to make breakfast. As I sip on my freshly brewed coffee and munch on a slice of toast, I allow my mind to wander, to imagine us back in Long Island, back where it all began.

But before I can dive too deep into my thoughts, my phone buzzes again.

An unknown number.

My heart lurches as I pick up, "Hello?"

A familiar voice replies, "Hello, Ella. It's been a while. This is Margaret Lovelace. You know, your grandmother."

I nearly drop the phone. Grandma? Calling me? Now? The universe certainly has a twisted sense of humor.

"Grandma Margaret?" I stammer, nearly dropping my toast on the floor. She hasn't called me in years. I don't think I've seen her since … the funeral.

We used to be close, but since I stopped visiting Long Island, we've drifted apart. I quickly recover my poise, putting on a bright tone. "Hi, Grandma. It's so lovely to hear your voice. How are you?"

"Oh, I'm just peachy, my dear," she says, her voice hearty and filled with warmth. "I wanted to check up on you. I heard through the grapevine that you might be coming back to Long Island for a visit."

The grapevine, also known as Mark. I should've known he'd tell her. And in record time, no less.

Mark and my grandmother had always had a special bond, much to my chagrin. I chuckle nervously, confirming her suspicion. "Yes, Grandma, Mark invited me to visit. It's been too long."

"Too long indeed, my dear," she muses, her voice sounding distant. "I still remember you both, two young lovebirds always running around the beach, laughing, not a care in the world."

Her words send a pang through my heart. I can see it so clearly, the sun-drenched memories of us on the sandy shores of Jones Beach, the music from the concerts still ringing in our ears as we laughed and talked into the late hours. "I remember too, Grandma. I miss those days."

"Then, my dear, it's high time you come back and make some new memories," she says, her voice brimming with conviction. "Long Island has missed you. I've missed you."

Her heartfelt words make my throat tighten. "I've missed you too, Grandma. I promise to come visit soon."

After a few more pleasantries, she gets down to business.

"Ella, my dear?" she asks.

"Yes, Grandma?"

"Remember that old bench along the boardwalk at Jones Beach State Park?"

I blush, even though she can't see me through the phone. Grandma wasn't there, but I know exactly what she's talking about. "I do," I reply. "Of course, I do. How could I forget?"

She chuckles knowingly. "If my memory serves me right, Mark once sat beside you on that bench and asked if you thought the two of you would still go there and sit together when you are old and gray. Am I recalling that story correctly?"

"You are," I say. "I've thought about that many times over the years."

"Well, dear, it sounds to me like it isn't over yet. Mark's wish might just come true … if that's what you want, too."

I smile. "I suppose you're right."

"Do you want to sit on that bench with him when you're old and gray, like me?" she asks.

The question is loaded because Grandma Margaret's lifelong love, my Grandpa Tim, passed away a few years ago. No doubt, she'd like to sit on that bench with him. He died suddenly, of a stroke. No one saw it coming. The two of them expected to have many more years together.

"If a second chance is in the cards for us," I say, "that would be lovely."

She sighs, and I can imagine what she's thinking.

We hang up, agreeing to chat more, in person. This conversation, coupled with Mark's unexpected invite, has made it abundantly clear that it's time to revisit the place and the people who used to be my world.

And for the first time in a long time, I feel ready. At least, I hope I'm ready.

Stepping into my home office, I begin working on emails for the upcoming week, but my thoughts keep wandering to Long Island, to the lapping waves and sun-kissed shores, to the home-cooked meals and laughter-filled nights at Grandma's, and of course, to Mark.

As I type away, I can't help but reminisce about those days, those memories that were once my everything. My mind conjures up images of Mark's wide grin, his ocean-blue eyes, the way his hand felt in mine as we strolled along the beach, the sound of his laughter as he joked around.

Before I know it, the day slips away, a blur of emails and nostalgic reminiscing. By the time I finish, the sky is tinted a beautiful orange, the sun beginning its descent.

And as I step outside, the warm evening air brushing against my skin, I can't help but think that maybe this trip to Long Island is exactly what I need. A chance to find closure, and who knows, maybe even a chance to rekindle an old flame.

Only time will tell. And until then, all I can do is hope that this leap of faith will lead to something beautiful.

I'm ready to face the past, ready to make new memories, ready to see what the future holds.

I'm ready to experience something truly beautiful.

A sense of calm washes over me. Long Island, here I come.

CHAPTER 19

MARK

Switching my brain from Ella and our impending trip to New York, I approach my training with singular focus. I'm Mark Dane, the professional athlete, one of the most prominent and recognizable faces of Nashville SC. I'm in the zone, and the zone is this concrete fortress of a gym, the musky scent of determination lacing the air, echoing with the clatter of weights and grunts of effort.

"Pain is weakness leaving the body, right?" I mutter to myself, yanking on my gloves with a tight grin. Peter is already waiting, a tower of muscle and patience. He nods at me, eyes a mixture of understanding and steely resolve.

The weight bar is cold and solid against my sweaty palms, its heft familiar and reassuring. Lifting it, I feel the familiar tension rippling across my muscles, feel the burn searing through me. My world narrows down to the bar in my hands and the count in my head.

One, two, three …

There's a rhythm to it, a cadence I've come to find soothing. Each curl, each press, each panting breath seems to push all thoughts of Ella out. For now. But her name echoes in my head, as persistent as my heartbeats, each repetition like an incantation that keeps pulling her image back—her blonde hair, that infectious laugh, those intense green eyes. But I push it down. I'm here to work, not daydream.

I feel the strain in my muscles, the creeping fatigue. Peter, ever watchful, motions for me to stop, but I shake my head. A few more reps. Just a few more. The bar becomes heavier, my breaths more labored, but I persist. This is what I live for—the push, the challenge, the triumph.

Finally, after what feels like an eternity, I drop the weights with a metallic clatter that reverberates through the gym. I'm breathing hard, sweat dripping down my face, but there's a sense of satisfaction thrumming in my veins.

"That's it," Peter says, clapping a hand on my shoulder. "Good job, Dane."

My legs feel like they've turned to jelly as I head for the showers. The warm water feels heavenly, washing away the sweat, the fatigue, the echoes of Ella that still linger in the back of my mind. As I scrub myself clean, my thoughts start to drift back to her, to New York, to the past that's waiting there.

I've dealt with tough games, brutal trainings, high-stakes matches. But opening old wounds—that's a different kind of challenge altogether. It's a game I'm not sure I know how to play. It's a game I'm not even sure I want to win.

After the shower, I dress and gather my things. My phone buzzes—a message from my friend Toby, asking if I'm free for a drink later. I type a quick reply and slip the phone back in my pocket, casting one last look at the gym. It's quiet now, almost peaceful. A stark contrast to the storm brewing within me.

As I leave, I feel a pang of ... something. Anticipation? New York looms ahead, a ghost from my past, from Ella's past. I have no idea what it holds for us, for me. But I know I have to face it. And I will.

As the saying goes, fortune favors the brave. And hell, if I'm anything, I'm brave. I know that much is true.

The day is drawing to a close as I head home, the sun dipping low in the sky, painting it with hues of orange and purple. It's a beautiful sight, but my mind is elsewhere. As I drive home, the cityscape of Nashville becomes a blur of lights and sounds, a backdrop to the drama unfolding in my mind.

It's going to be an interesting trip, that's for sure. As I park my car and head inside my house, I chuckle.

"Buckle up, Mark Dane," I mutter to myself, "You're in for one hell of a ride."

I kick off my shoes and settle into my couch, and a calm settles over me. The day's end finds me mentally preparing for what lies ahead. In the quiet of my home, surrounded by familiar things, I allow myself a moment of vulnerability. A sigh escapes my lips as I close my eyes, the image of Ella, vibrant and laughing, the last thing I see before darkness takes over.

Tomorrow is another day, another step closer to our reunion, another chapter in our story. But for now, I push those thoughts aside, let the fatigue take me. The last thing I remember is the soft hum of the city outside, a lullaby that ushers me into a restless sleep.

The scene is set, the players ready. New York, Ella, the past—they are waiting. And so am I.

The next morning, the new day blooms with the promise of a fresh start. Sunlight pours through the gaps of my blinds, creating a pattern on the polished hardwood floor of my Nashville home. Rousing from the lull of sleep, I blink my eyes open and sigh. I'm sprawled on my couch, a fact I attribute to my dazed thoughts from the night before.

Ella. She's everything anymore.

The surge of anticipation returns in full force, electrifying the otherwise languid morning. With a groan, I push myself up, muscles stiff from the uncomfortable position, and my gaze falls onto the unopened sports drink on the coffee table.

Shaking off the remnants of sleep, I take a swig of the drink before trudging towards the kitchen, barefoot and clad in my soft, worn-in tee and shorts.

As the scent of fresh coffee wafts through the air, filling the house with a comforting aroma, my mind drifts towards Ella again. Her laughter, the spark in her eyes, the way her nose crinkles when she's amused—it all dances at the edge of my consciousness.

I sound like a broken record. *Ella, Ella, Ella.* I can't help myself.

A soft chime resonates in the serene morning,

jolting me from my thoughts. It's my phone, lying abandoned on the counter from last night.

A text from Toby flashes on the screen, confirming our drink … for last night.

Shit. I completely forgot. What kind of shitty friend am I?

Damn.

My fingers fly over the keys as I reply with a short apology before tossing the phone aside. I ask if we can meet up today, instead. I'll need the distraction, something to tide me over the relentless march of time until I see Ella again.

Toby will understand. I know he will. When the phone chimes again, I already know it's him, agreeing to a do-over today.

Making myself a quick breakfast of scrambled eggs and toast, I allow the monotony of the task to lull my thoughts into silence. Once plated, I carry my meal towards the floor-to-ceiling window.

The view is breathtaking, the Nashville skyline coming alive under the golden morning light. The city stretches in all its grandeur, an urban landscape humming with life and rhythm. I lose myself in the sight, forkfuls of food absentmindedly making their way into my mouth.

Once finished, I rinse my dishes and place them into the dishwasher. The mundanity of the task grounds me. But as I climb the stairs to get ready for the day, each step feels heavy. It's as if I'm moving closer towards a precipice, a dive into a past filled with Ella, and the anticipation is heady.

The spray of the shower does little to shake off the encroaching thoughts of her. *Ella.* Her name is like a mantra in my head, a rhythmic chant that resonates with every beat of my heart.

It's as if she's everywhere—in the warmth of the water cascading down my skin, in the rich scent of my soap, in the soothing hum of the water against the shower tiles. I can't escape her, and honestly, I don't want to.

Freshly showered and dressed, I can't shake off the anticipation. With every tick of the clock, every passing hour, I'm one step closer to her. The past and present are intermingling, dancing a complicated tango in my mind.

Back in my bedroom, I pause at my window, looking out at the city humming with life. A few short days will bring a different view, a different city, and most importantly, Ella. My heart does a strange flip at the thought.

For the rest of this day, I lose myself in the hustle of life, in the noisy camaraderie with Toby over drinks, in the normalcy of my daily routine. It's a welcome distraction, a way to reign in the thundering anticipation for the upcoming trip.

By the time I return home that evening, the city is bathed in the glow of the setting sun, casting a beautiful orange hue over Nashville. Inside the sanctity of my house, I stand in the silence, caught in the tide of thoughts surging within me.

My mind dances between apprehension and excitement. Soon, I will see Ella again. Soon, I will confront our demons. Soon, I'll set foot in New York, walking back into a past I left behind, now painted in shades of her.

And so, I welcome the night, each passing moment bringing me closer to the dawn of a new chapter.

Soon, Ella. I promise, my voice echoing in the quiet room. As I close my eyes, her image fills my vision. I surrender to the serenity of sleep, my dreams a playground for the exciting days to come.

The night brings with it a promise of the reunion, the revelations, the return to New York. And as I succumb to the pull of sleep, I know that the coming days will bring with them an adventure.

CHAPTER 20

ELLA

Three Days Later

The incessant ding of my phone alarm snaps me out of a whirlwind of fragmented dreams and into the stark reality of my present life. It's the day Mark and I travel to New York. I run my hands through my disheveled hair, trying to disperse the sleepiness.

A quick glance at my alarm clock shows me it's barely 5 am. The sun hasn't even peeked over the horizon. My phone vibrates with an incoming text message. It's from Mark.

Ready for our adventure, sleeping beauty?

His humor-filled text makes me chuckle. This man, even before dawn, knows how to bring a smile to my face. I quickly respond.

Always ready for adventure, especially with my handsome prince.

As I rise from bed, the excitement from recent dates

with Mark still clings to me, wrapping me in a cocoon of happiness. I head to the bathroom and catch a glimpse of myself in the mirror. My green eyes shine brighter than they have in ages, and my heart seems lighter, almost hopeful.

After a quick shower, I slip into a breezy sundress and flat sandals, fitting for the mid-summer New York heat. I twist my hair into a loose bun and put on minimal makeup—a hint of mascara and a splash of lip gloss.

Walking down the stairs, I pause for a moment to take in the silent townhouse. It feels like the calm before the storm, a silence that wraps around me like an old friend.

The scent of freshly brewed coffee wafts from the kitchen, welcoming me. After pouring myself a cup, I add a dash of cream and swirl it around. My gaze lingers on the creamy waves as they ripple through the rich darkness of the coffee. It's a comforting ritual that brings a sense of normalcy to the otherwise unusual day.

A soft chime pulls me out of my thoughts. Another text from Mark.

I'm outside.

The rush of adrenaline hits me like a tidal wave. This is it. The beginning of our trip back to our roots, back to Long Island, where it all began. I grab my carry-on bag and sling my purse over my shoulder.

Clara has offered to check in on Gonzo while I'm gone. She already has a key, so I quickly scrawl down some instructions and leave them on the kitchen counter. His care is easy, really. I'm sure she can handle things while I'm away.

The door creaks slightly as I open it, releasing a soft gust of early morning air that tickles my skin. Mark's standing by his sleek black car, looking every bit as handsome as ever. His Nashville SC cap sits casually on his head, sunglasses perched on top, and his broad shoulders lean against the car door. His face lights up as he spots me, a warm smile gracing his face.

"Ready?" he asks, as he takes my bag, his gaze meeting mine. His eyes, deep pools of blue, seem to sparkle in the early morning light.

I nod, a mixture of excitement and trepidation bubbling within me. "As I'll ever be," I answer, offering him a smile that matches his own.

As we pull out of my driveway, I glance at my townhouse, my sanctuary. A mixture of fear and anticipation swirls within me. We're heading back to a past that has left its scars, back to a place filled with memories that simultaneously made and broke us.

Yet, as I gaze at Mark, who's focused on the road, a sense of calm envelops me. We may be delving into our painful past, but we're doing it together. The unknown doesn't seem as terrifying when he's by my side.

As the morning starts to lighten, the first streaks of the sun painting the sky in a beautiful hue of orange and pink, I feel the tension ebbing away. Today is the beginning of the next stage in our journey together, a step towards healing our old wounds. With that thought, I lean back in my seat and close my eyes, allowing the hum of the car and the rhythm of the road to lull me into a tranquil silence.

When we arrive at the Nashville airport and enter the terminal, I can't help but imagine the homecoming awaiting us on Long Island. There are familiar places to see, family to hug, and a past to face. Yet for now, in the cocoon of the dawn light, I revel in the silent comfort of our shared memories.

As we board the plane and settle into our seats, I intertwine my fingers with Mark's. Maybe I'm too much of an optimist, but I can't help it. I know that whatever awaits us, we'll face it together.

There's no turning back.

We're on our way to Long Island, back to the past, and hopefully, towards a future together. I close my eyes, and just as I did on the car ride to the airport, I allow the hum of the engine to lull me into a tranquil silence.

Little do I know, it's going to be a day filled with surprises and discoveries, taking us on a roller coaster of emotions. For now, I let the anticipation build, adding another layer to this trip.

I can hardly wait to see what unfolds next.

The thrill of traveling, of leaving behind what's familiar, has always held a certain allure for me. It's almost as if, up in the air, suspended between cities, everything else fades away, leaving only the journey, and the closeness of Mark beside me.

After an uneventful flight, we land at LaGuardia, and the first thing that hits me is the heat. It's a different kind of heat than Nashville—thicker, more oppressive, the humidity lingering in the air like an unwelcome guest.

Mark and I collect our luggage and order an Uber to drive us to Long Island.

He's quiet during the ride, his gaze lost in the blur of cityscape whizzing past our windows, his fingers drumming an absent rhythm on his jean-clad thigh. I sense his anxiety. New York is his past, his hometown. This trip is dredging up a whirlpool of emotions, and even though he's holding it together, the strain is evident.

While the car cruises over Queensboro Bridge, a spectacular view of the city unfurls before us. The sight of the towering buildings against the backdrop of a cloudless sky stirs something within me. A pang of nostalgia—no, more than that, a sense of homecoming.

New York, for all its noise, chaos, and teeming millions, was where I grew into the person I am today. My college years were some of the best of my life, even though Mark broke my heart.

I sigh as I gaze out the window, deep in thought.

The remainder of the ride to Long Island is filled with sporadic conversation, most of it initiated by me. I ask Mark about his old haunts, and he obliges, pointing out landmarks and narrating childhood anecdotes with a wistfulness that makes my heart ache.

Once we arrive at the cozy B&B in Bay Shore, we check into our rooms. The place is super cute, overlooking Seaborn Marina and near Seatuck National Wildlife Refuge. It looks like a comfortable place to spend quality time.

I'm surprised and oddly pleased when Mark hands me the key to my own private room. I arch an eyebrow at him, and he gives me a boyish grin in return. "I thought we could take things slow, you know? No pressure."

Relieved, I find myself smiling back at him. Even though we have rekindled our romance, sleeping in the same bed might have felt too sudden, too soon. It's a sentiment I find incredibly touching.

Before we part ways to freshen up, Mark adds, "Meet me in the lobby in an hour? I've planned a little surprise for you."

Curiosity piqued, I nod, watching him saunter off to his room. I allow myself a few minutes to bask in the warmth of our reconnection before heading to my own room. The excitement bubbles up within me, almost tangible, almost like a secret shared between lovers.

My room is small and quaint, the decor a delightful mix of rustic charm and modern elegance. The antique bed is layered with fluffy pillows and a plush comforter, and the view from the window is a picturesque landscape of lush greenery. Everything is immaculately clean and tidy. I love it. I freshen up, eager to explore the town.

Just as I'm finishing, a text buzzes in. It's from Becca.

HOW'S THE TRIP?

I GRIN, imagining the wide-eyed curiosity in her voice.

· · ·

GOOD SO FAR. Mark is ... amazing. It's like we never spent a day apart.

THERE'S A PAUSE, and then she replies.

YOU DESERVE all the happiness in the world, Ella. Enjoy your trip, and keep me posted!

TOUCHED BY HER MESSAGE, I text back a quick thank you and tuck my phone into my purse. It's comforting to know that while I'm in a different city, uncovering layers of a past relationship, life goes on as usual in Loveland. Ever After Bridals is in safe hands.

As the hour Mark asked me to wait for nears its end, I grab my purse and head down to the lobby. The butterflies in my stomach are fluttering with an intensity that surprises me.

This is Mark, after all.

The same Mark who was my best friend before he was my boyfriend. The same Mark who has seen me in my best and worst lights. Yet, there's an undeniable thrill, a sweet anticipation of the unknown that's making my heart race.

Whatever awaits me in the lobby, whatever memories we'll revisit here on Long Island, one thing is clear. This is a journey we are embarking on together, a path we've chosen to walk side by side.

I breathe in deeply, gathering my thoughts, and push

open the door to the lobby. This is just the beginning, and I can't wait to see what unfolds next.

CHAPTER 21

MARK

The air felt electric as Ella and I arrived at the idyllic bed and breakfast overlooking Seaborn Marina. Our rooms, and our separate worlds for the night, waited for us like untouched canvases. The place is cozy and inviting, an emblem of rustic charm and character, making the world beyond its walls seem irrelevant, like a distant memory.

"Wait for me in the lobby, Ella," I told her, the hint of a surprise shimmering in my eyes. "I've got a little something planned for you." Her emerald eyes sparkled with curiosity and she nodded, the corner of her lips twitching upwards into an intrigued smile.

As she headed to her room, I caught a glimpse of her in the soft light of the lobby—her tousled, sun-kissed hair, her light summer dress that floats around her like a dream, and her eyes, a captivating mix of curiosity and excitement.

It's moments like these that make me feel like the luckiest man on earth.

Turning to Mrs. Sullivan, the venerable matron of the B&B, I confirmed the arrangements. "The boat's ready, Mrs. Sullivan?" I asked, the low timbre of my voice barely rising above a whisper. She nodded, her eyes twinkling with understanding. This was going to be the perfect surprise for Ella.

I stepped outside, taking a moment to appreciate the sun casting long shadows over the marina. The air was alive with the soft squawk of seagulls, the comforting sounds of the sea a soothing balm on my taut nerves. The boat, waiting patiently at the dock, was a simple yet elegant affair—small and intimate, a perfect setting for the surprise I have in mind.

Now, returning to the lobby an hour later, Ella is waiting as I'd asked her to.

She is the picture of serene beauty, the afternoon light dancing in her eyes and playing off the edges of her tousled hair. The sight of her fills me with an emotion I can't quite put my finger on, but it feels a lot like home.

"Well, ready for the surprise?" I ask with a playful grin.

She smiles back, her eyes sparkling with … dare I say it? *Love* for me.

I reach out and tuck a loose strand of hair behind her ear, my fingers lingering for a moment longer than necessary. There's a familiar charge in the air, a tension that feels both new and exciting. But right now, it's time for surprises and shared moments, a chance to further unravel the complexities of our relationship.

As we prepare to set off for an evening under the

starlit sky, the soft whisper of the wind carrying the promise of an unforgettable night, I feel so damn grateful.

Grateful for the past, for the present, and for whatever the future holds for us.

Thank you, I say under my breath, to no one in particular.

The rest of the chapter and our time in New York still lies ahead of us, a tale yet to be woven, a story yet to be told. But for now, as I lead Ella to the awaiting boat, I enjoy watching our story continue to unfold, one beautiful moment at a time.

The clink of Ella's sandals has my pulse ticking like a metronome, marking time to an intimate rhythm only we seem to comprehend. The radiant glow in her eyes mirrors my excitement, hinting at the surprise waiting in the wings.

Underneath my playful exterior, though, my nerves hum like a bassline, low and steady. I'd be lying if I said her expectations didn't make me sweat.

Honestly, I've learned in my years of, let's call it manhood, that if you don't feel a little dizzy from nerves and anticipation, you're not playing the game of love right. And right now, I'm the dice, the board, and the player, all rolled into one.

All bets are on.

Mrs. Sullivan shoots me a conspiratorial glance that does nothing to ease my nerves. The mischievous gleam in her eyes screams that she's in on the secret.

Bless her heart.

See? I sound like a real Nashvillian.

"Boat's ready, dear," she croons, her voice floating over to me like a lullaby, painting pictures of romantic ventures on moonlit waves. Her words pull me back to the task at hand and the surprise I have planned for Ella.

Before I can think twice, I find myself outside again, the smell of brine and seaweed wafting through the air, nudging me back to the present moment. As I look at the boat bobbing gently in the calm marina waters, my heart races like a wild stallion, untamed and unpredictable.

The setting sun graces the sky with warm hues, and the marina takes on the golden glow of a painting too perfect to be real.

Just when I think my heart can't race any faster, it does. Ella blushes and raises one shoulder, the golden sunlight playing off her tousled hair like an ethereal halo. In that moment, I feel an invisible thread tugging at my heart, pulling me towards her like a moth to a flame.

"Ready for your surprise?" I ask, my voice carrying the playful undertone that has become our shared language.

She looks at me, curiosity dancing in her eyes, and I can't help but fall in love with her all over again.

As I reach out to tuck another stray hair behind her ear, my fingers brush against her skin, setting off a string of electric sparks between us. Our connection, as thrilling as it is reassuring, blankets us in its familiarity, a silent affirmation of the bond we share.

Being here, on Long Island, intensifies those feelings.

Slowly, I extend my hand to her, the unspoken invitation hanging in the air like a promise. Her fingers slip into mine, her skin soft and warm, fitting into my grip as though made for it. A soft smile plays on her lips, and I return it with a smile of my own.

Leading her to the boat, I relish the soft sound of the waves, the smell of the ocean, and the anticipation that fills the air. Our fingers remain intertwined, and the world seems to disappear around us, leaving only the two of us and the promise of an unforgettable evening.

As I help her aboard, her fingers brush against my chest, sending a warm rush coursing through my veins. My heart skips a beat as our gazes lock, her emerald eyes reflecting the dusky sky, glistening with stars and untold stories.

Ella, oblivious to the full extent of the surprise waiting for her, looks at me with sparkling eyes full of trust. I return her gaze, my heart pounding. This evening, just like the past few days, is a piece of our shared narrative that's still being written.

As we slowly drift into the serene beauty of the evening, the boat bobbing gently on the moonlit waves, I am awed by the excitement that tingles in the air. Tonight, away from the daily grind of Nashville, away from the prying eyes and well-intentioned worries of friends, we are creating a world that is ours and ours alone. A world of shared secrets, of memories that have yet to unfold.

Under the starlit sky, the silence around us is as soothing as it is profound. Our pasts may be riddled with heartbreak, but right now, here under the vast expanse of the sky, we are in a bubble, untouched by time and unmarred by the world.

As the night deepens, our shared silence becomes a comforting lullaby, filling the air with a sweet sense of tranquility. Ella's fingers squeeze mine, her touch both electrifying and soothing.

"Whatever the surprise is," she whispers, "I know I'm going to love it. I already do."

Her words warm my heart, and I squeeze her hand in return, my mind buzzing. Little does she know that this is just the start of our adventure, a small taste of the emotions that are yet to unfold.

A lot can happen in one night under the stars.

CHAPTER 22

MARK

My heart pounds like a drumline in my chest as I steer the boat, sneaking sidelong glances at Ella. Her eyes, glinting with anticipation, dart between the horizon and me, a puzzle she's eager to solve. I can't help the smug grin curling my lips, thriving on the suspense I've masterfully crafted.

Not to mention, it feels good to be back on the water. I've missed this.

As the boat slices through the silky current, the moonlight and starry canvas overhead serve as our only sources of illumination. They cast an ethereal glow onto Ella, painting a picture more enchanting than any I've seen. She's a living work of art—a marvel of nature that takes my breath away every time I look at her.

"Almost there," I say, elongating my words, basking in her impatience. She huffs, rolling her eyes but the smile on her lips betrays her amusement.

When Jones Beach Theater comes into view, I can feel the jolt of surprise that shoots through her. It mirrors my own from that night, years ago when fate, or some cosmic power, brought us together.

A band is playing on stage, their music dancing on the breeze and wrapping us in an acoustic embrace. I kill the engine and let the boat bob on the gentle waves, letting the magic of the moment saturate the air around us.

Ella turns to me, surprise morphing into an emotion I'm beginning to recognize as something more. Her eyes glisten under the celestial glow, and I feel a jolt of triumph for having brought that look into them. It's a moment frozen in time, a bubble of bliss in the chaos of life, and it's all ours.

"Mark, this is ..." she trails off, her words carried away by the wind.

It doesn't matter. I understand.

Some sentiments need no words, and this is one of those times. We exist in a universe of shared silence, the rhythm of our hearts providing the only soundtrack we need.

I reach out, my fingers finding hers. It's a dance we've engaged in often, and yet, each time feels like a revelation. Our hands entwine as naturally as our lives have, a testament to the connection that runs deeper than either of us could have anticipated.

A gust of wind picks up, rustling Ella's hair, fanning it around her face like a halo. The sight of her, illuminated under the moonlight, is enough to send my heart galloping even faster.

A beautiful chaos. A mesmerizing paradox. That's what Ella is to me.

"What do you say we dance?" I ask, disentangling our fingers to stand.

Her eyebrows lift in amusement. "Here?"

"Here," I confirm, extending my hand towards her, feeling the thrumming anticipation in my veins. She takes my hand, allowing me to pull her up and into my arms. We sway to the music, our bodies finding a rhythm as unique as our connection, our laughter lost amidst the symphony of the sea and the distant concert.

We dance, and as the music washes over us I lean in, my lips brushing her ear. "I can think of no better place, no better moment, and no one else I'd rather be with," I confess. She pulls back, her eyes searching mine, and then she's reaching up, her fingers curling behind my neck, drawing me down to meet her kiss.

The world blurs as our lips meet, the world outside our little bubble ceasing to exist. It's just us, the moonlight, the serenade of the distant music, and the rhythmic lullaby of the sea. Our hearts beat in sync, a testament to the beautiful, undeniable bond that connects us.

The kiss deepens, passion seeping into it, coloring the moment with shades of love that are still new to us. We break apart only when the need for air overpowers us, our foreheads resting against each other, our breaths mingling in the narrow space between.

Lauren Daigle is on stage, singing her hit song "Thank God I Do" about how grateful she is to have her love in her life. The lyrics are a perfect summary of how Ella and I feel about each other.

Tonight, under the same stars where it all began,

our relationship has crossed a significant milestone. We're in deeper than we'd ever imagined, the uncharted territory as thrilling as it is terrifying. But if Ella's soft smile and the look in her eyes are any indication, it's a journey we're both willing to embark on.

Soon, we can't resist temptation any longer, and it feels like all of my dreams are coming true. I've imagined this moment so many times. So many ways. Each of them perfect, just like Ella.

We grab each other and kiss hungrily as clothes fall haphazardly onto the damp floor of the boat. The night air feels electric as we explore each other's bodies, relishing the familiar while also being curious about what's new.

This woman feels like home. I mean it. *She feels like home.*

When she's in my arms, I feel safe and loved and whole in a way I've never experienced with anyone else before. Not to mention, she thrills me. How many other women own elegant bridal boutiques but also have pet snakes?

Ella's a one of a kind. I want her to be mine ... again. Forever, this time.

I look up at the stars and say a silent prayer to the universe, asking it to be so.

For what feels like hours, we make sweet, passionate love. It's incredible. The connection we have is all I'll ever need.

Later, as we return to our seats, basking in the afterglow of the lovemaking and the music, I feel a deep sense of contentment. Ella nestles into my side, her head resting on my shoulder.

But beneath the calm surface of my contentment, a niggle of unease stirs, uninvited. I've left a significant part of my past unresolved, a ghost that threatens to infringe upon the blissful present.

A ghost that goes by the name of Sylvia.

For now, I push the unwelcome thoughts away, focusing on the woman beside me and the memory we've just created. Tomorrow is another day, and with it will come its own challenges. Tonight, it's just Ella and me, surrounded by the place and the music of our beginnings, a shared memory etched under the watchful gaze of a thousand stars.

As the concert concludes and the final notes of the last song drift across the bay, I realize that the stage is set for a new act. Little do I know, the curtain will rise sooner than I think. And when it does, I'll have to face the music in more ways than one.

With Ella's hand securely in mine, I start the engine, steering us back to the dock at the B&B, to the heart of reality. Tomorrow's dawn promises a new day, a new scene, and a confrontation I'm not yet ready for. But as the old saying goes, tomorrow is another day. I only hope it's a day that won't tear us apart.

The stinging salt air whips through my hair as I navigate the boat back toward the shore. The rumbling of the engine beneath me feels like a mighty, primordial heartbeat. My skin is slick with sea spray, and my eyes squint against the brilliance of the moon's reflection dancing on the waves.

Beside me, Ella is nestled into the corner of the bench seat, a bright smile playing at the corners of her lips. Her eyes are closed, her brow smooth in a rare moment of pure, unadulterated contentment. With her wild curls tousled by the wind and the silver moonlight setting her skin aglow, she is ethereal, a mythical sea nymph brought to life.

I'm tempted to keep this peace, this silence that's so full of unspoken words, but the story of us remains unfinished and I'm itching to turn the page. Our past is a narrative that has been paused for eight long years. It's time to hit play again.

"Ella," I say, my voice barely audible above the humming of the engine and the gentle lapping of the waves against the boat.

Her emerald eyes flicker open, meeting mine. There's a light in them, warm and inviting, that ignites a familiar spark in my chest.

"Do you remember when we first met?" I ask. My words are laced with nostalgia, seasoned with a dash of humor to lighten the gravity of the conversation. It's our past we're dredging up, after all, not the Gettysburg Address.

Ella laughs, a sweet, melodic sound that rings through the night air, mingling with the nocturnal symphony of the sea. "At the Jones Beach Theater?" she replies, her words colored with the hues of fond memories.

"Yep," I say, a smile of my own unfurling on my lips. "Eight years ago. We were just a couple of college kids, chasing the summer sun."

She nods, her eyes misting over with distant memo-ries. "And you were the handsome soccer player who was too good to be true," she adds, teasing me with a playful wink.

"Ah, but I was real," I retort, feigning offense. "And I still am. Real, that is."

"I know you are," she says, her voice softening. "And you've turned out to be so much more than I ever expected."

Her words hit me like a physical blow, searing through my chest and burning a path straight to my heart. We've moved so far beyond the realm of soccer and sun-kissed beaches. Our bond, once severed, has grown stronger, more potent with the passage of time.

"I want you to know something, Ella," I say, my voice firm, resolute. "I may not be that college kid anymore, but my feelings for you ... they haven't changed."

She's silent for a moment, her eyes reflecting a universe of emotions. She's quiet, but her silence is eloquent, teeming with unspoken words and hidden meanings.

"And what about you?" I ask, holding my breath as I wait for her response. "Have your feelings changed?"

Instead of answering, she leans in closer, her body pressing against me as she wraps her arms around my neck. Her lips brush against mine in a whisper of a kiss, light as a feather but heavy with promise.

"My feelings for you are as strong as ever, Mark Dane," she says, and my body goes all gooey from happiness.

"Good."

The echoes of our past and the uncertainty of our future blend into a beautiful paradox in this moment. The story of us is far from over, but for now, we have this. This shared memory, this shared space, this shared kiss. And it's more than enough.

As we pull away, I see a soft blush coloring her cheeks. She bites her lower lip, a telltale sign of her nervousness. "We should head back," she says, her voice shaking slightly. I nod, respecting her decision to end the moment on her terms. It's time to head back, after all.

And tomorrow, I promise myself, we'll write another chapter in our story. One day at a time.

The engine roars back to life, the boat skimming the water surface with newfound determination. But as I guide us back to shore, I feel a prickling of nervousness. We're headed back, yes, but we're also moving forward. On to whatever comes next.

The theater and its nostalgic memories fade into the distance, replaced by the twinkling lights of the town of Bay Shore and the looming structure of the B&B where we're staying. I secure the boat and help Ella onto the dock.

Tonight, we've opened the door to our past. Now, it's time to face the real world, to face our present and all its realities.

And I'm ready. Ready to fight for this second chance, for this renewed bond that's somehow stronger than it ever was. Ready for whatever Ella throws my way. Ready for our future together.

The sound of the rolling waves fades into a

comforting lullaby, wrapping us in a shared sense of nostalgia and hope.

As we head towards the inviting warmth of the B&B, I cast one last glance at the moonlit sea. It's quiet now, the surface calm and serene, holding within its depths the promises of tomorrow.

Later, back at the B&B, the warmth of the evening unfolds around us like a velvet quilt, the moon high in the sky casting long, ethereal shadows on the sandy edge of the bay. Ella and I are ensconced in foldable chairs, toasting the night with a bottle of rosé, cocooned in the peaceful hum of cicadas and the gentle murmur of the water against the shore.

I glance at Ella, her eyes twinkling in the moonlight like distant galaxies. There's a quiet thoughtfulness to her gaze that makes my heart twist uncomfortably. I've always been good at reading her, a skill honed during our special summer and one that, evidently, hasn't rusted over time.

I decide to lighten the mood, joking, "Are we classy enough yet with the rosé, or should I have brought caviar?"

Her laughter peals through the quiet night, a sound so bright and genuine it paints the darkness with shades of joy. "Mark, your metaphors are just as crazy as your soccer dribbles," she teases, a lightness in her tone that eases my heart.

As the wine ebbs lower in the bottle and the night deepens, our conversation meanders down memory lane. We talk about youthful pranks, midnight jamming sessions, and the wild parties where we first fell for each other. We avoid talking about the end, though. About the misunderstandings and hurt feelings that tore us apart. That will come later, I know.

"El," I start, swirling the dregs of my wine, "I was thinking ... maybe it's time we have a conversation about ... us."

Ella's gaze snaps to mine, her eyebrows furrowing just slightly. "Us?"

I nod, running a hand through my hair. "Yeah. Us. And what happened eight years ago. And Sylvia."

Ella's face pales at the mention of Sylvia, my ex-girlfriend and the wedge that drove Ella and me apart. "What about her?"

I sigh, knowing this isn't a conversation I can put off any longer. "I never got closure. With Sylvia or with us. She's still on this island, probably still furious, and that could cause problems. Not just for me but for us ... if there's going to be an us."

Ella's quiet for a long time, the cicadas and the lapping of the water against the shore filling the silence between us. When she finally speaks, her voice is soft but determined. "Mark, I'm not scared of Sylvia. And I'm not scared of us. But if we're going to do this, we have to be honest. No more running away, okay?"

I find myself nodding, a sense of relief washing over me. "Okay, Ella. No more running. Except on the soccer field, that is."

The tension of the conversation ebbs away, replaced by a newfound understanding. I hope, anyway. I don't want to assume, but I want so badly for this to work.

As we make our way inside, my mind is filled with

thoughts of the days ahead. With Sylvia's looming presence on this island and the unresolved tension between Ella and me, I sense the stirrings of a storm.

But that can wait. For now, for tonight, I allow myself to hope.

CHAPTER 23

ELLA

The morning after the boat ride is a study in contradictory emotions.

A delicate excitement sits in my chest like a secret too precious to share, and yet a seed of unease takes root in the back of my mind, watered by Mark's unexplained absence. I awaken in the tangle of white cotton sheets, the scent of him lingering like a faint melody, the bed next to me cool and empty.

He spent the night in my room last night. We made love ... again.

Yet now, he's gone.

He left a simple note, saying he'd catch up with me later. I almost wish he hadn't. I don't know what to think it means.

After a quiet breakfast of homemade scones and raspberry jam alone in the quaint dining room of the B&B, I decide to explore Bay Shore, to lose myself in the charming town and perhaps in the process silence the nagging sense of uncertainty that's started to curl its tendrils around my heart. Because after all, I didn't come to New York to sit in the room by myself.

Strolling down Main Street, the world is drenched in the full bloom of summer. Flowers nod their colorful heads in window boxes, their sweet scent wafting on the breeze. I spend the morning drifting in and out of boutique shops, the sounds of the town wrapping around me like an old, comfortable blanket.

There's an easy rhythm here, one that's a familiar echo of those past summer days spent in this part of the world eight years ago.

After a lunch of shrimp po' boy at the local café, I find myself walking back to the B&B, a swirl of thoughts accompanying each footstep. The day is perfect, bathed in the gentle glow of nostalgia and the comforting thrum of the present, but without Mark by my side, it feels incomplete, like a beautiful painting with a crucial element missing.

I could call or text him, but I don't want to appear desperate.

I won't chase him down. That's not my style.

As I approach the entrance to the B&B, a figure steps out from the front door, and my heart lurches in surprise. It's Sylvia, with her wavy chestnut hair and that dimpled smile. The same Sylvia who once claimed Mark's heart. She recognizes me instantly, her eyes widening for a fraction before she composes herself, the ghost of surprise replaced by an unsettling nonchalance.

"Ella," she greets, her voice a ripple in the tranquility of the afternoon. She looks different and yet achingly the same, her eyes reflecting a maturity that the passing years had evidently bestowed.

"Sylvia," I return, struggling to maintain my composure. We engage in small talk, the past sitting heavily between us like an unwanted guest. Each passing moment unravels new layers of discomfort, my earlier unease taking form in the shape of Mark's ex-girlfriend.

The questions in my mind multiply, rapid and insistent like a hummingbird's wings. Why is she here? Does Mark know? Does he still care? Is this why he wanted to come back here? I know too much, but also, maybe not enough.

The exchange is brief, yet it leaves a lasting impact, like a stone thrown in a still pond.

As Sylvia walks away, her parting words echo in my mind. "It's nice to see you again, Ella."

The sincerity in her voice is disconcerting, throwing me further off balance.

Inside the B&B, I make my way up the stairs, each step heavy with the weight of my questions. Mark's door is still shut, the silence behind it resonating louder than any spoken words.

I close the door of my room behind me, sinking into the cushioned chair by the window.

Outside, Bay Shore continues to live its tranquil, rhythmic life, oblivious to the storm brewing in my mind.

Mark and I have been picking up the scattered pieces of our past, attempting to build something new, something beautiful. But the emergence of Sylvia introduces a factor I hadn't considered. An unresolved chapter from Mark's past. A chapter that includes me but is not entirely about me.

My thoughts return to the note he left, a vague explanation that now seems deliberately evasive.

As the day fades into a dusky twilight and Mark still doesn't return, my resolution hardens. I need to talk to him, to understand his past … our past. There are missing pieces in the puzzle of our relationship, and I owe it to myself and to us, to complete it.

The longer he's gone, the more pronounced his absence feels. His laughter and his warmth become a void that echo my growing apprehensions.

Finally, he texts, asking me to meet him for dinner. Somewhat reluctantly, I agree. I have to find out where he's been, and with whom.

Later, the evening settles over Bay Shore like a velvet curtain, the sky awash with hues of indigo and stars peeking through. Underneath this celestial canopy, Mark and I find ourselves at a little Italian restaurant, its low lighting and vintage decor a nod to the Old World charm.

Tonight, though, the atmosphere feels less romantic, more akin to the calm before the storm. The shadows thrown by the flickering candlelight are a mirror image of my own turmoil.

Mark's voice has the timbre of a question mark, the words floating uncertainly between us, "You've been quiet, Ella."

His gaze is steady, the clear blue of his eyes reflecting the soft glow of the candles. The dimples that usually accompany his smile are absent, replaced by a subtle tension etched on his face.

He's noticed my unease, my silence.

I force a smile, buying a few seconds before responding, "Just ... a lot on my mind."

A semi-truth. I've never been one for confrontation in my romantic relationships, preferring to dodge the storm rather than weather it. But tonight, the storm needs to be faced. That's what we've come to New York to do, after all.

Before I can gather my thoughts, the waiter approaches, breaking the tenuous silence with his offer of the house special—fettuccine alfredo. We place our orders, the mundane action providing a momentary distraction from the looming conversation.

With the waiter gone, I gather my courage, the words taking shape on my tongue. "I ran into Sylvia today."

There. I've said it.

The syllables hang in the air between us, like the faint strains of an out-of-tune violin. I watch as Mark's expression shifts, a ripple of surprise swiftly overtaken by a furrowed frown.

"She came by the B&B?" His voice is guarded, the familiar humor absent.

I nod, my fingers tracing the condensation on the side of my water glass, the cool droplets grounding me. "Yes. She said it was nice to see me again," I add, my voice steady despite the whirlwind of emotions inside.

Mark looks down at the table, his fingers tapping a restless rhythm against the edge. He is silent for a few seconds that stretch like elastic, taut with unspoken words and unasked questions.

"Ella, there's something I should've told you before," he finally speaks, his voice a low rumble that is almost lost in the murmur of the restaurant.

It's happening. The unraveling of stories, the surfacing of hidden truths.

My heart flutters in apprehension, nervousness swirling in my stomach like the pasta we're yet to eat.

"Alright, Mark," I say, a soothing note to my voice, attempting to lighten the moment, "I'm all ears."

He chuckles, a brief flash of his typical buoyancy. But his smile doesn't reach his eyes, and that's when I know. We're about to plunge into uncharted waters. To navigate through the foggy terrain of his past.

Here we go.

As Mark begins to unfurl his past, the clatter of dishes and the hum of chatter from other tables fades into a blurry soundtrack. His voice becomes the only sound I'm tuned into, each word etching a story that intertwines his and Sylvia's lives.

"I met Sylvia in high school," he starts, his fingers twisting around his silverware. There's a somber note to his voice, an underlying melody of regret that sends a shiver through me. "We dated through my first year of college. I thought … I *thought* I was in love."

There's a heavy pause, filled with the ghosts of heartbreaks past. I remain silent, letting him tell his story at his own pace.

The sting of jealousy is sharp, unexpected. I've

known of Sylvia, of course, but hearing about their history makes it all the more real. It makes it tangible.

Mark's voice continues to weave the narrative. "When we graduated from high school in Oyster Bay, I moved to Massachusetts to attend Boston College and pursue my soccer career. Sylvia stayed here in New York. The distance was hard, and then when I came home for that summer after freshman year, I ... I met you, Ella."

I swallow, my throat suddenly dry. The memory of our summer love affair seems so vivid, a stark contrast to the faded murals of his past with Sylvia. I reach across the table, my hand covering his. His fingers are warm, grounding me in the present.

"But I left you, didn't I?" His voice is a mere whisper, the question rhetorical. I pull my hand back, wrapping my arms around myself as if to keep the hurt at bay. "Sylvia and I tried again, but it was never the same. When you love someone, and you leave them for someone else, it changes things. It changed me."

His confession hangs in the air, a shroud of past mistakes and regret. The honesty in his words, the rawness of his emotions, strikes a chord in me. I thought I was prepared to hear his story, but now, immersed in the harsh reality of his past, I find myself floundering.

"So, Sylvia ...?" I probe, unable to complete the question.

"She's part of my past, Ella," he says firmly, meeting my gaze with a solemnity that sends a wave of relief through me. "I need to face it, to resolve things. But I don't want it to ruin what we have now."

I draw in a deep breath, his words echoing in my mind. His past with Sylvia, his unresolved issues, they're like a puzzle piece I hadn't known was missing. And now, with it in place, the picture is clearer. More complicated, perhaps, but undeniably real.

But there's something else. Something more. I can feel it.

I have no choice but to let Mark tell me … when he's ready. I must let this thing play out. What other option do I have?

I pause, a heavy silence surrounding us.

"Alright," I finally respond, my voice barely above a whisper. "Alright, Mark."

We sit there, in the softly lit restaurant, a universe of words unsaid and feelings unraveling. The pasta arrives, the aroma wafting through the air. But the knots in our stomachs, wound tight with heavy revelations and profound conversations, have little room for food.

The rest of the evening is a blur. The Uber ride back to the B&B is filled with silence, a quiet understanding passed between us. When we finally reach our separate rooms, the weight of the night's revelations settles heavily around us.

But there's a sense of catharsis too. We've delved into uncharted territory, faced the shadows of the past, and come out on the other side.

Now, I wait.

CHAPTER 24

MARK

The first light of dawn is filtering through the threadbare curtains of my room at the B&B, staining the room in a soft, muted gold. The quiet, the solitude, it's a stark contrast from the vibrant energy that had filled the same space last night.

I'm still in bed, a crumpled sheet haphazardly thrown over me, the taste of the previous night—of Ella—still lingering.

The memories are heavy, almost tangible as they coil around me. I can still feel the echo of her laughter, the warmth of her body pressed against mine. Eight years have passed, but being with Ella feels as familiar as breathing. The world might have moved on, but it's as if Ella and I are forever trapped in the heart of that one summer here on Long Island, when love felt like an adventure, a thrilling discovery.

Reaching out to the bedside table, I grab a bottle of water, letting the cool liquid wake me from the lingering haze of sleep. In the peaceful silence of the early morning, I allow my mind to drift back to that summer.

The summer of us.

The college days, when we were young and reckless and in love. Ella, with her golden hair and electric energy, had stolen my heart without even trying. We would spend days at the beach, our laughter mingling with the crash of the waves. Nights were spent exploring local pubs and talking about our dreams under the starlit sky.

But in the background, a phantom was always looming—my past, my unresolved feelings for Sylvia.

When I had broken things off with Ella, I thought that I was making the right decision, returning to a relationship that had once been comfortable and predictable. I'd been an idiot to think I could settle for that after experiencing the whirlwind that was Ella.

Returning to Sylvia had been like drinking flat soda —familiar but unsatisfying. The chemistry that I'd once thought we had seemed to fizzle out, replaced by the dull throbbing of regret. I had traded the fireworks I'd had with Ella for the comfort of familiarity with Sylvia, but all I'd ended up with was the bitter taste of remorse.

I'd tried, though. I'd really tried to convince myself that Sylvia and I could go back to the way things had been. But every laugh felt hollow, every conversation was dull.

Letting out a sigh, I glance at the digital clock on the bedside table. It's still early. Ella is probably still asleep in her room, a mere wall away. The need to talk to her, to explain further, is strong. But the fear of her reaction is stronger.

I don't know if I'm ready to open this can of worms. Not yet.

I might be a professional soccer player who is confident on the field, but my heart is delicate when it comes to my true love.

Pushing the thoughts away, I get up from the bed, my muscles protesting. The lack of exercise is catching up to me. I'm in dire need of some training, a shower, a cup of strong coffee, and a game plan.

As I do some push-ups in my room and get ready for the day, I steel myself for the confrontation that is bound to happen. I need to tell Ella more about Sylvia, about the part of my past that's still unresolved. But most importantly, I need to convince Ella—and maybe even myself—that what happened eight years ago is not who I am today. I'm no longer the confused kid who broke her heart.

As the shower water cascades over me, washing away the remnants of sleep, I know what I have to do. It's time to prove to Ella that I'm not that guy anymore. I'm ready to show her that the Mark who broke her heart eight years ago is not the Mark standing in front of her today.

And as I step out of the shower, towel wrapped around my waist, I know that this is just the beginning. The past is about to meet the present, and I can only hope that it's ready for the collision. As I look at my reflection in the steam-fogged mirror, I wonder if I'm ready too.

Only time will tell.

I can only pray that Ella is ready for the ugly truth.

To tell this story, I have to take you back to those summer days, when the air was filled with the smell of salt water, suntan lotion, and the unbridled freedom that comes with being young and in love.

Ella and I had an indescribable bond, one born from an unspoken understanding that we were meant for each other. That summer, we basked in the warm embrace of love, and everything else ceased to exist.

It was us against the world.

Yet, in the midst of this passionate summer romance, I found myself gravitating back towards Sylvia. Maybe it was familiarity or the shared history that drew me back, but it wasn't the same. The love I had for Sylvia, once so vibrant and all-consuming, now seemed like a flickering candle compared to the roaring fire that was my love for Ella. It was like trying to fit a square peg into a round hole. I was torn between my past and my future, and the consequences of this indecision would prove to be more than I bargained for.

One day, in the midst of this chaos, I got a call from Sylvia. Her voice, trembling with fear and anxiety, broke the news.

She was pregnant.

My world came crashing down around me. Here I was, a college student barely able to take care of myself, let alone a child.

I felt a wave of nausea wash over me, a cocktail of fear, guilt, and dread. I could hear my heartbeat in my ears, pulsating like a warning siren. But in the background, I could hear something else. The sharp, gut-wrenching sound of my heart breaking. The child wasn't just the product of my past. It was a living, breathing symbol of my betrayal to Ella.

As I grappled with this news, I made the difficult decision to leave Ella. Not because I stopped loving her, but because I loved her too much to drag her into my mess. I tried to go back to Sylvia, to make things right, to play the role I was suddenly thrust into. But nothing was the same.

My heart was with Ella, but my duty was with Sylvia.

The remainder of that summer became a blur of hospital visits, doctor's appointments, and sleepless nights. It was a cruel twist of fate that in my attempt to escape my past, I was being pulled back into it with a force that left me breathless.

And then, as suddenly as it all started, it ended. Sylvia lost the baby. A profound sense of relief washed over me, immediately replaced by a wave of guilt for even feeling relieved.

In the aftermath of that heartbreaking time, Sylvia and I drifted apart. I returned to college in Massachusetts, carrying the weight of my guilt and regret with me. But through it all, I never stopped loving Ella. The thought of her was my only solace, the only thing that kept me from completely losing myself.

I was too ashamed to ever contact her.

Now, as I sit in the B&B, the echoes of that drama reverberate through my mind. The fear, the guilt, the loss. But most of all, the love. The love I have for Ella, the love that has survived time and distance, heartbreak, and loss. It's this love that now compels me to tell her everything.

She deserves to know the truth.

As I walk towards her room, my heart beats erratically in my chest. The stakes have never been higher, but the time has come for me to face the entirety of my past decisions. I stand before her door, take a deep breath, and knock. It's long past time to reveal the secrets I've held onto for far too long.

I owe Ella the truth. And she deserves nothing less.

I ask her to come to brunch with me, so that we can talk some more. She agrees to meet me there, although I sense her reluctance.

Maybe I'm making too big a deal of this. Maybe she expects me to tell her something worse than the truth. Maybe she's built it up in her mind to be far more terrible than it actually is.

I don't know. This is a mess.

I'm a mess.

Later, seated at a window table overlooking a bustling outdoor patio, it's as if the world outside the cafe knows what I'm about to do. The sky is a somber, uniform gray, a sharp contrast to the vibrant colors of the local area I've come to love.

The cafe is walking distance from our B&B, and Ella said she'd be here soon.

I glance at my watch. Five more minutes.

The silence in my mind is deafening, my heart pounding like a drum solo at a rock concert. But the decision is made. I've decided to embrace the full measure of my past mistakes, and hope that somehow, some way, Ella will understand and forgive me.

I take one last gulp of my coffee, which has grown lukewarm, the bitter taste reminding me that things will get difficult before they get better. The chime above the cafe door rings out, cutting through the hushed whispers of the customers around me.

I turn, and there she is.

Ella. Beautiful, enchanting Ella, dressed in a soft cream blouse that brings out the golden hues of her hair. Her green eyes are wide and questioning. She gives me a hesitant smile, but I can see the traces of uncertainty flicker in her gaze. I rise to greet her, my heart an erratic symphony in my chest.

"Hi, Ella." I manage to get the words out, hoping my voice doesn't betray the storm brewing inside me.

"Mark." She returns the greeting, the uncertainty now replaced with a forced cheerfulness. I guide her to a chair and sit opposite her, feeling the weight of what I'm about to reveal.

"You look lovely," I tell her, because it's the truth, but it's also easier than starting the conversation we need to have. She thanks me, twirling a lock of her hair around her finger, a nervous habit I've come to associate with her when she's anxious.

"Thanks," she says, followed quickly by, "Are we breaking up again?"

"What?" I ask. "No. I mean, I don't think so. Are you interested in that MindMate guy you were with the night we bumped into each other in Nashville? Is that what this is about?"

"No. I'd thought about it, but no," she says. Her gaze is probing, questioning. "Were you with *her*? You've been away, and I haven't known where. Is she coming between us again? Because I won't—"

"No," I say, before she can finish her thought.

"Okay," Ella replies, but I can tell she's worried.

"I asked you here because … because there's something I need to tell you, Ella." My voice is shaky, a poor cover for the storm beneath my seemingly calm surface.

Her eyes grow wide. "Mark, what's wrong?"

The moment of truth is upon me. "Ella, you remember Sylvia, right?" I ask her, carefully gauging her reaction. Her face turns pale, and she nods. "That's the woman you're referring to."

"From your high school, yes, I remember …" Her voice trails off, and I know she's putting the pieces together. "But wait. You know I remember. I saw her yesterday. Why are you asking like this? You're acting weird. It's freaking me out."

"She was pregnant, Ella. That summer when I broke things off with you … she was pregnant with my child." The words come out in a rush, my heart squeezing in my chest as I watch her face.

Her reaction is swift and immediate. Her eyes widen in shock, her mouth falling open slightly. I watch as she swallows hard, taking a moment to compose herself before she speaks.

"And you're just telling me this now?"

I shake my head, my hands clenched tightly on the table. "It's complicated. I tried to rekindle things with Sylvia …"

Ella's quiet for a moment, her eyes scanning my face for any signs of deception. When she finally speaks, her voice is soft, filled with a mix of disbelief and pain.

"And the baby …?"

"The baby didn't make it. Sylvia had a miscarriage." My voice is barely above a whisper. Ella closes her eyes for a moment, processing the information. When she finally looks at me, her eyes are a whirlpool of emotions —pain, confusion, shock, but also maybe … understanding.

"Mark, why are you telling me this now?"

"Because I want to be honest with you, Ella. I don't want any secrets between us. I love you, and if we're going to have a future together, I want it to start with a clean slate."

I look into her eyes, hoping she sees the sincerity in mine.

She doesn't respond immediately, her gaze dropping to the table as she ponders over my words. Her silence is deafening, making my heart pound even harder in my chest.

This is it—the ultimatum. She can walk away, and I wouldn't blame her. Or she can choose to stay, to fight through this with me.

Ella looks up at me then, her eyes shimmering with unshed tears. "Mark … I …" She trails off, her gaze drifting to the window. The world outside continues to move, oblivious to the crossroads we're standing at.

"Take your time, Ella," I tell her gently, reaching across the table to squeeze her hand. I feel her hand tremble beneath mine, but she doesn't pull away. As I sit there, holding her hand across the table, I can only hope that our past won't dictate our future.

"You love me?" she asks.

"Isn't that obvious?" I reply. "Absolutely, I do."

The cafe fades away around us, the buzzing conversations, the clatter of dishes, the scent of fresh coffee, everything is secondary. There's only Ella, her eyes filled with a mix of emotions, the silence between us heavy with decisions yet to be made.

As she takes a deep breath, ready to speak, the world outside the cafe seems to hold its breath with her.

CHAPTER 25

ELLA

The next morning, sunlight filters through the delicate lace curtains, flooding the room with a warm, dappled glow.

I awaken in the quaint B&B bedroom, the bedding beneath me crisply white and oddly impersonal. The room smells faintly of lavender and wood polish—comforting but too sterile, too untouched. It lacks the essence of lived-in comfort.

My eyes wander to the unoccupied space in the bed beside me, and I can't help but feel a pang of sadness. Just a few feet across, but it might as well be miles.

The space between us feels like an insurmountable chasm, fraught with words unsaid and secrets finally revealed.

The mirror on the wall reflects back a woman caught in a whirlwind of emotions, her eyes a little too bright and her heart far too heavy. The familiar freckles dotting my skin look like constellations in an unfamiliar sky.

The truth about Mark, Sylvia, and the baby they almost had—they're not just suspicions or shadows anymore. They're as real as the pulse that beats in my veins. But beneath the hurt, beneath the waves of confusion crashing over me, the love I have for Mark remains unshaken.

I need clarity, guidance, and perhaps a cup or two of wisdom-infused tea. There's only one place that can offer me that. Dressed in a breezy sundress and armed with my favorite sunglasses, I call an Uber, ready to escape to Massapequa and seek solace in the warm embrace of Grandma Margaret's home.

The ride is a silent one. I watch the world whizz past me—a blur of lush greenery and warm summer skies. Every mile closer to Grandma Margaret's house offers a sense of comfort. Her house is more than a building. It's a sanctuary of warmth and memories, a beacon that always welcomes me with open arms.

As I step out of the car, I'm greeted by the familiar sight of her house—timeless and comforting. My heart unclenches just a bit, a sigh of relief escaping my lips. The scent of blooming roses mixed with Grandma Margaret's famous apple pie wafts from the open windows, playing a gentle melody of homecoming.

Her welcoming smile is the same as always. Her hair, a little grayer than when I saw her last, is tied in a neat bun, and her glasses hang low on her nose. She's a woman from a different era, her life woven with threads of wisdom and experiences. And right now, I need that wisdom more than anything.

We spend the morning reminiscing about the past—happy times, challenging moments, and the unforgettable summer when Mark became more than just a friend. He became my world.

Her voice, soft and rhythmic, is a balm to my frayed nerves, her stories painting a picture of the girl I used to be and the woman I've become.

Over cups of her special chamomile tea and slices of warm apple pie, we delve into the complicated situation with Mark and Sylvia. She listens with a calm demeanor, occasionally patting my hand in a silent show of support. My heart feels lighter with every word I spill, the burden of untold secrets easing off my shoulders.

As the conversation comes to an end, I find a semblance of clarity within the chaos.

Mark might have made mistakes, but so have I. Our love isn't perfect, but then again, whose is?

I think it's a battle I'm willing to fight.

I look at the pictures on the wall—decades of memories marked with love, pain, and perseverance. They're proof that love can conquer all, even the most heartbreaking truths.

With a renewed sense of purpose and a heart full of gratitude, I get ready to leave. I'm not just the girl who fell in love with Mark anymore. I'm a woman ready to fight for that love.

As I step back into the Uber, I know what I need to do next. I need to talk to Rosie and Clara, to share everything and seek their support. Together, we'll figure out how I can navigate the rough waters I find myself in.

At least now, I know what I want. I know where I stand.

The Uber ride back to the B&B is a blur of mixed emotions. As we pass by the sandy beaches and the kids playing on the boardwalk, I remember the times when life was simpler, when love was a summer fling and heartbreak was only a fleeting moment. But I'm not that girl anymore, and I realize that I've got bigger battles to fight.

Arriving back at the B&B, the old Victorian house appears more imposing than ever. Its quaint charm somehow feels deceiving, like an alluring facade hiding a labyrinth of secrets. My heart thumps in my chest as I walk up the path. The coming conversations are going to be hard, but necessary.

As I unlock the door to my room, I steal a glance at Mark's room. A sense of determination settles within me. No matter how challenging things get, I have to remind myself of one thing. Mark is worth it, and so is our love.

I draw a deep breath, steadying my nerves. It's time to call Rosalie and Clara, and unravel the tangled threads of mine and Mark's intertwined destinies.

For someone who prides herself on her words, I'm struggling to articulate mine. I gather my thoughts, trying to find the best way to unravel the tumultuous tale that has become my life.

Rosalie and Clara are quiet, waiting. After a deep breath, I begin.

"We made love again," I start, and then it all pours out.

The boat ride, the evening spent reconnecting, the depth of the emotions that surprised even me. I talk about the electric moments and the heart-wrenching ones, the secrets revealed, and the ones yet to be explored. I speak of Sylvia, the unborn child, the pain and the confusion. My voice wavers, but I continue, the words tumbling out in a rush.

There's a continued silence on the other end of the line as my story concludes. I can almost visualize Rosalie and Clara, sitting miles away, digesting it all. I feel bare, my heart exposed, but it's liberating too, to voice it all, to have my truths hanging in the air.

It's messy, it's complicated, but it's real.

Then, Rosie speaks. Her voice is soft, but it carries the strength I so desperately need. "Sweetie," she says, "love isn't a bed of roses. It's full of thorns, but it's those thorns that make the roses worth it. Just look at what Patrick and I went through before settling into happiness together. Mark … he's your rose, isn't he? He's different from all those other guys you've been distracting yourself with. Different from the meaningless flings and one-night stands. He fell in love with the real you, back before you were a badass bridal boutique owner and prominent fixture in the Loveland community."

A lump forms in my throat. I swallow hard, blinking back the tears. I know she's right, and for the first time, I allow myself to fully accept it. "Yes," I whisper. "He is my rose. He is different from all the others. So very different."

There's a pause as we all shed a tear, then Clara's pragmatic voice breaks into the emotional moment. "Alright, so we know you love him. We know he's worth fighting for. The question is, what's the plan, El?"

And just like that, the conversation shifts from the emotional to the practical. For the next hour, we brainstorm, dissecting each element, considering all possibilities. Rosie and Clara provide insights that I wouldn't have thought of, offering solutions, hope, and most importantly, unwavering support.

As the call finally comes to an end, I realize the night has fallen, wrapping the world in a blanket of inky darkness. The room feels less empty, less lonely, their voices still echoing in my ears. With a plan forming in my mind, I know what needs to be done.

Mark's past might be a maze, but I'm willing to navigate it, to fight through the thorns for my rose.

The first step of my plan? It's time to confront Sylvia, to bring light to the shadows of the past that have been haunting us. For love, for Mark.

Laying back on my bed, I stare up at the ceiling, my mind a whirl of plans and possibilities. The path ahead won't be easy, but for the first time, it seems less intimidating, more feasible. I feel a familiar warmth spreading through me.

I can do this. Surely, I can do this.

As the moonlight filters in through the window, casting a soft glow on the room, I know that a new chapter is about to begin, a chapter where I'm not just a bystander, but the one taking charge. For now, the plan is clear. Sylvia is the first step on my path to reclaim the love that was lost and a future that could be ours.

With my mind teeming, I turn off the lights.

The last thought in my mind before sleep claims me is a silent vow to myself. For Mark, for us, I won't back down. Not anymore.

CHAPTER 26

MARK

The next day, the afternoon light streams through the window of my room at the B&B, casting playful shadows on the old hardwood floor. I stand before the mirror, examining my reflection. This is a ritual I've followed since childhood.

It's a strange, private tradition.

I hate that Ella and I are spending so much time here on Long Island without spending it together. It seems like a shame. I'm lonely without her.

My gaze lands on my eyes—deep blue like the coastal waters of New York—and I see a man tangled in webs of decisions, one foot stepping towards the woman he loves, the other hesitating over the ghost of a past he can't shake off. I scrub a hand over my stubble, a prickly reminder of the sleepless night before. I think of Ella and how her fingers gently grazed my cheeks just days before.

Ella. Her name is a balm to my restless soul, a salve to the open wounds of my past.

Just as I'm about to peel off the shirt I've slept in, the sound of a car pulling up into the gravel parking area out front interrupts me.

A familiar sight, one that sends my heart into an anxious dance. It's Charles Dane, himself. *Dad.*

I quickly don a fresh shirt, glancing one last time at my reflection before heading out to greet him.

I descend the staircase, each step matching the rhythm of my racing heart. The fragrance of cinnamon and baking bread wafts from the kitchen, a comforting, homey aroma that does little to ease my anxiety. I swing the front door open just as Dad steps out of his sleek, black car, a stark contrast to the vibrant greenery of the Long Island summer.

His eyes, mirror images of my own, crinkle into a warm smile. Dad's hair, once a rich chestnut like mine, is now a distinguished salt and pepper. He carries his age with an air of wisdom, a silent testament to the years he has spent navigating the highs and lows of life.

"Son," he greets, wrapping me in a firm hug. The familiar scent of his aftershave is a rush of nostalgia, memories of baseball games and fishing trips flooding back.

"Dad," I respond, matching his grip.

We make our way inside the common area of the B&B, settling in the cozy living room. As I pour some coffee, the comfortable silence between us is disrupted by the unspoken questions hanging in the air.

He's quiet for a while, sipping his coffee, before he finally breaks the silence. "How are things with Ella?" he asks. The tone of his voice is casual, but I know him well enough to catch the undercurrent of concern.

I sigh, resting my cup on my knee. "It's ... complicated."

"Isn't it always?"

He chuckles, but there's a seriousness in his gaze.

I take a moment, gathering my thoughts, deciding how much to reveal. He waits patiently, understanding my need for him to take this at my pace.

"I told her about Sylvia," I admit, my voice barely above a whisper. The weight of my confession hangs heavy between us.

His eyebrows lift in surprise. "And?"

"And I don't know." I run a hand through my hair, frustration gnawing at me. "I don't know where we stand. I don't know what to do next."

He's still for a moment, considering my words. Then, with a sigh, he places his cup on the coffee table and turns to face me fully. "Mark, love isn't about doing the perfect thing. It's about doing the right thing. And only you can decide what that is."

I smile at his words. They're a reassurance I didn't know I needed. A green light in the maze of my confused emotions. Perhaps it's time I confront my past once and for all. Perhaps it's time I face Sylvia.

Maybe I need to apologize to her before I can move on.

As the sun climbs higher in the sky and the day warms, I realize this could be the turning point in my relationship with Ella. But before I can step into that future, there's something I need to do. A plan forms in my mind, a path to a possible resolution.

"Dad," I start, relief surging within me. "I need your advice on something. I have a plan that could potentially change everything."

Dad pauses mid-sip of his coffee, his eyebrows raise inquisitively. Light streams in through the open window, illuminating the living room, yet doing nothing to dispel the anxiety that clings to my words.

My plan, albeit simple, is daunting. A confrontation with Sylvia, a resolution to a chapter that has been left open for too long. It's a path riddled with uncertainties and potential heartbreak. Yet, it's one I'm willing to walk, if it means a future with Ella.

"I want to meet with Sylvia. To clear the air, once and for all," I lay it out, my gaze not leaving Dad's.

He sets his coffee down, leaning back in his chair, his eyes reflecting a complex mix of surprise, concern, and understanding. There's a pause, the seconds ticking by as I wait for his response.

"Mark," he finally speaks, his tone measured, careful. "Are you sure about this? Sylvia … she's … well, she's not the easiest person to deal with, if memory serves me right."

I nod, a rueful smile pulling at my lips. "Trust me, I know. But I also know that if I want any chance of a future with Ella, Sylvia cannot be an unanswered question between us."

His gaze softens, a touch of pride flashing in his eyes. "You really love her, don't you? Ella."

I take a deep breath, letting the truth of my feelings for Ella fill the room. "More than I ever thought I could love anyone. She's my future. I'm sure of it."

Dad is silent for a moment, a sense of understanding passing between us. Then, he nods, offering his support. "Alright, son. Let's set this up. Sylvia needs to hear your side of the story, too. Let's clear the air. It will be better for everyone."

I feel a surge of relief at his words. "Thank you, Dad." There's so much more I want to say—gratitude for his support, fear of the uncertainty that lies ahead, hope for what might be. But all that comes out is a simple thank you.

As Dad gets up to leave, promising to make some calls and set up an impromptu dinner at his place in Oyster Bay for this evening, I'm left with a mix of anxiety and resolve. This is a step I need to take, for Ella, for myself.

Later, when Ella comes out of her room for some food, I relay the plan to her. She's taken aback, apprehension flickering in her eyes. But after a moment, she nods, her hand finding mine. "Okay, Mark. If you think this is what we need to do, I'm with you." I squeeze her hand in gratitude.

She seems relieved, as if she, too, seeks resolution. This is good.

And so, as the day progresses, we prepare for the evening that could very well redefine our lives.

We invite Grandma Margaret to join us for support. We don't know how this dinner will turn out, what

Sylvia might say, what emotions may surface. But as I look into Ella's eyes, a sense of mature determination resonates between us.

We're in this together. And somehow, that makes everything seem less daunting.

CHAPTER 27

ELLA

It's an evening filled with unknowns as I stand at the threshold of Charles Dane's home, Mark's hand securely wrapped around mine.

His father's house is a beautiful two-story beachfront property in Oyster Bay. The sea breeze carries the comforting scent of the ocean, its calming whispers enveloping us as we step out of Grandma Margaret's car.

Charles, a handsome, distinguished man in his sixties, greets us at the door with a warm smile. "Ella, Mark," he nods, guiding us into a home that mirrors the sophistication and warmth of its owner.

It's been years since I've seen Mark's dad, but it feels like no time has passed at all. I always liked him.

The living room flows into an open-concept dining area. The table is a long, mahogany piece surrounded by cushioned chairs, and is already dressed in a crisp, white tablecloth. The dining area is dominated by a grand bay window, showcasing a panoramic view of the water beyond. Crystal glasses and polished silverware catch the last of the sun's rays, casting prismatic rainbows onto the walls.

As we help set the table with a variety of delectable dishes ordered from a local catering company, a sense of surreal calmness washes over me. Is it possible for such an average setting to hold so many pivotal moments?

The chiming of the doorbell breaks the silence, our collective breaths hitching at the arrival of the missing piece of this puzzle. *Sylvia.*

Mark stiffens beside me, his grip on my hand tightening as he heads towards the front door. I exchange a quick, reassuring look with Grandma Margaret, her calming presence a welcome respite.

To everyone's surprise, Sylvia steps out of a sleek, silver Volvo SUV with a man by her side and two children, their shared features undeniably prominent.

Wow. I didn't see that coming.

Relief visibly washes over Mark's face as he takes in the sight before him. This unexpected twist to our dinner had been unbeknownst to us, and Sylvia's introduction of her family opens a path to a peaceful resolution.

"Ella, Margaret, Charles," Sylvia begins, her voice softer than I remember, "I'd like you to meet my husband, Jeremy, and our kids, Ava and Liam."

Mark's gaze meets mine, his eyes holding a silent conversation, echoing the unspoken understanding that Sylvia has moved on, just like him. Her husband, a handsome man with warm eyes, greets us with a cordial nod, his arm securely wrapped around Sylvia's waist.

As we continue with light conversation, I can't help but recall the absence of a wedding band on Sylvia's hand when we ran into each other a few days prior. Casually, I bring it up, only to have Sylvia laugh it off. "I'd been playing tennis earlier that day," she explains, "It was in my jewelry box at home."

Following some more pleasant conversation, Mark stands, his chair scraping against the floor and breaking the room's comfortable hum. He looks at Sylvia, his gaze steady, "Sylvia, could you join me in the kitchen, please?"

A wave of unease sweeps through the room as we watch Mark lead Sylvia away. It's a defining moment, a culmination of old hurts and new beginnings. His hand briefly squeezes mine before he leaves, a silent promise of closure.

In the quiet hum of the dining room, I let out a slow breath I hadn't realized I was holding.

It's not long before they return, Sylvia's face softer, Mark's eyes brighter. "I apologized for the past," Mark begins, his gaze never leaving mine, "Sylvia and I, we're okay now."

Sylvia nods, placing her hand on her husband's. "We've moved on, Mark. We're happy. It's okay for you to do the same."

And for the first time that evening, I truly breathe. The past, it seems, is finally ready to rest.

After an evening filled with unexpected twists, the house quietens. The hushed sounds of a friendly card game between Charles and Margaret drift from the living room.

Mark and I step outside into the crisp night, enveloped by a star-studded sky that stretches into infinity above us. We find ourselves on a wooden bench overlooking the waterfront, the rhythm of the waves echoing the pulsing heartbeat of the world around us.

I pull my legs up onto the bench, curling into Mark's side as he wraps an arm around me, his warmth a tangible comfort. His scent, a mix of sea salt and masculinity, wafts around me, grounding me in this moment of intimacy. We sit in companionable silence, the sounds of nature around us, the lights from the house painting a surreal picture.

"I want to tell you something," I begin, my heart thumping. Mark turns his head to me, his eyes glinting with the reflection of the distant stars. "I've had my fair share of lovers over the years," I admit, a blush creeping into my cheeks under his steady gaze, "but none of them meant anything, you know?"

I can see the understanding in his eyes as he gives me a slow nod, urging me to continue.

"Looking back, I think I was waiting for you," I confess, my voice barely a whisper against the lull of the sea. Mark's body tenses beside me, his breath hitching. I press on, laying my heart bare, "No one else ever measured up. No one else was you."

In the silence that follows, I can hear my own heartbeat, a steady rhythm that mirrors the rise and fall of the ocean waves. Before long, Mark breaks the silence, his voice raw and filled with an emotion that tugs at my heart. "I've been waiting, too," he says, his gaze dropping to our entwined hands, "Hiding behind guilt, avoiding relationships, because deep down I knew it was you. Only you."

A wave of relief washes over us both, the weight of unspoken words lifting off our shoulders. We sit there, looking out at the calm sea, a silent agreement passing between us. It's time to let go of the past and embrace the love that's been quietly blooming over the past eight years.

We talk about how fate or maybe the universe conspired to bring us back together, the random encounter at a Nashville bar transforming into a second chance at love. I tell him about the MindMate date that led me there, how I was tired of meaningless relation-ships and yearned for something real.

And that night, I found it. I found him.

Our conversation ebbs and flows, a rhythm that mirrors the rise and fall of the waves on the shoreline. We talk about our past, the summer love that was cut short, a rehearsal for the real thing that was yet to bloom. We talk about the present, our hearts beating in tandem, a testament to the depth of our emotions.

And finally, we talk about the future. Our future.

As the night deepens, we make our way back to the B&B, our bodies moving in silent agreement. The passion between us grows, fueled by years of longing and love. We lose ourselves in each other, the world fading away until there's just us.

The lovemaking is good. Oh, so good.

In the quiet aftermath, we lay tangled in the sheets,

our hearts beating in sync. A new day dawns, and with it comes the promise of a new beginning.

We pack our things, our hearts brimming with a love that's stood the test of time.

As we check out of the B&B and fly back to Nashville, we make plans to combine our lives, to build a future together. A promise of a love story that's only just beginning.

Sure, there are plenty of real-world trials and tribulations to face. For starters, I'll need to find out how repairs are going on The Romantics building. I hope renovations can resume soon. I'll also need to continue work on my new bridal line and be ready when Sonny and his camera crew want to focus on Ever After Bridals. Not to mention, I'll need to fill my parents in on my visit with Grandma and reintroduce them to Mark.

But with Mark—my Mark, from all those years ago —I'm home. It might sound simple, but he's everything to me. Our life, together, is everything to me. This is our second chance. Our happily ever after. The details will work themselves out.

Forget Wes and MindMate. Forget casual sex with Javier, and all the others. Forget pretending to be interested in men who I'm not.

Finally, this is my sweet surrender. I am completely, totally, and unapologetically myself. And Mark loves me, for me. In all of my contradictions.

I'm the luckiest girl in the world.

"Mark?" I ask after the plane touches down in Nashville.

There's a focused silence as us weary travelers wait for the captain to announce that we can unbuckle our seatbelts.

"Yes, my love?"

"Do you remember that bench? At Jones Beach. That one time …?"

He smiles broadly and takes my hand. "You know, I do. How could I forget?"

"Do you remember what you asked me as we sat there together?" I ask.

He leans over and kisses me gently on the forehead. "We'll be there. Old and gray, and still together. I can hardly wait."

EPILOGUE

MARK

8 Weeks Later

The Nashville sunset paints the sky in hues of pink and orange as I steer the car towards our destination, the soft hum of the engine filling the air. Ella sits in the passenger seat, her eyes focused on the changing scenery. A crisp autumn breeze drifts through the slightly open window, carrying with it the tantalizing aroma of dried leaves and the promise of change.

"Isn't it crazy," I begin, my eyes never leaving the road ahead, "how guilt can transform into such a monstrous thing? Yet, forgiving, airing things out, and letting go ... it's all so simple. It can happen in a flash."

My heart swells at the thought of Ella and the winding road that brought us back to each other. I glance at her, her profile illuminated by the soft glow of the setting sun.

Her laughter fills the car, a melodious sound that tugs at my heartstrings. "Life has a funny way of teaching us lessons, doesn't it?" she remarks, turning towards me. Our gazes lock for a moment, an unspoken promise of love passing between us.

We're happy. Genuinely happy.

We fall into a comfortable silence, our thoughts revolving around the plans for our new house in Loveland and the life we are building together. My temporary move to her townhouse feels like a prelude to our upcoming domestic bliss. The excitement bubbles inside me like a wellspring, the thrill of a new beginning pulsing in the air between us.

Although we haven't spoken it out loud, we're both excited to make our union official. There's no one else. There never will be.

This is it. She's my world.

As the skyline of Nashville and then the familiar shape of Geodis Park comes into view, Ella looks at me, a hint of confusion in her gaze. "Mark, the season is over. There's no game tonight," she comments, realizing where we're heading. "What's up?"

I smirk, keeping the surprise to myself.

Her face lights up as we enter the stadium, a look of utter disbelief replacing the confusion. The lights are on, a small crowd is gathered around the goal post. It's a mixture of our friends and family.

The sight of my dad and Grandma Margaret brings a soft gasp from Ella. They came all the way from New York. Rosie and Patrick, Clara and Sean, Becca, Rachael,

Toby, Peter, Ella's parents, Coach Henderson, and many other familiar faces turn towards us, their smiles as bright as the stadium lights.

"What is all this?" she whispers as she gently nuzzles my ear.

"You'll see," I reply with a smile.

As the crowd parts, I lead Ella towards the center. Under the bright lights, I take a deep breath, sinking to one knee, my heart pounding in my chest. "Ella," I begin, my voice loud and clear, "I've brought you here, to a very special place, for a very special reason. My forever true love, will you marry me?"

The silence is deafening as the world seems to hold its breath.

"Yes!" she says, making me the luckiest, happiest man alive.

The moment Ella utters the word "yes", the PA system erupts in loud cheers, the lights flashing in celebration.

I'll have to thank our operations guy who helped me pull this off. I owe him. Big time.

I slide a diamond solitaire onto her finger, and it sparkles under the stadium lights. Pride swells in my chest, and I can hardly believe she's really mine.

A familiar melody fills the air, the sweet tune of Lauren Daigle taking us back to the night on the boat under the stars. Lauren sings about how she doesn't know who she'd be without her love. I don't know who I'd be without mine. Thank God, I have her. I do.

With Ella in my arms, we dance under the open sky,

our hearts beating in sync with the rhythm. It's magical. But this night is also about fun for everyone who's here to share in this momentous occasion with us. When our slow dance is done, the music changes to a faster beat, and the stadium transforms into a celebration of love and togetherness.

Ella laughs, twirling in my arms. I know, in my heart of hearts, everything is right in our world.

Laughter, joy, and music fill the air as our loved ones savor the moment along with us.

The journey that led us to this day might have been paved with heartaches and misunderstandings, but it also brought us back to each other. As I look at Ella, her eyes sparkling brighter than her diamond engagement ring and all the moonlight on the New York sea, I know.

One day soon, we'll be pronounced Mr. and Mrs. Dane. This is the beginning of our forever.

THE END.

* * *

Get the next book in the series:

Tie the Not

ABOUT THE AUTHOR

STANDARDS OF STARLIGHT BOOKS
KELLY BRIGHT

Blissfully in love with her real life Prince Charming for a quarter century and counting, Kelly Bright knows a thing or two about happily ever after.

She believes love conquers all and that there's someone special out there for every single one of us. She writes emotional, feel good romantic comedy.

When her head isn't buried in a romantic book or movie, you'll likely find Kelly with Mr. Bright—scoping out charming settings for her next story or chatting up other meant-to-be couples and learning how they met.

Connect with Kelly at BrightHappyLove.com, and

on Instagram, Facebook, and TikTok at @brighthappylove.

www.ingramcontent.com/pod-product-compliance
Lightning Source LLC
Chambersburg PA
CBHW061440210726
48287CB00007B/2295